N

FATHER OF THE ORPHANS

The Story of Janusz Korczak

JEWISH BIOGRAPHY SERIES

FATHER OF THE ORPHANS

The Story of Janusz Korczak

MARK BERNHEIM

FOREWORD BY KATHERINE PATERSON

illustrated with photographs

LODESTAR BOOKS   E. P. DUTTON   NEW YORK

Library of Congress Cataloging-in-Publication Data

Bernheim, Mark.
  Father of the orphans: the story of Janusz Korczak / by Mark
Bernheim.
    p. cm.—(Jewish biography series)
  "Lodestar books."
  "Korczak's works in English": p.
  Summary: A biography of the Polish doctor, author, founder of
orphanages, and promoter of children's rights, whose life, though
swept away in the Nazi holocaust, was dedicated to his love
for children.
  ISBN 0-525-67265-6
  1. Korczak, Janusz, 1878–1942—Juvenile literature. 2. Jews—
Poland—Warsaw—Biography—Juvenile literature. 3. Educators—
Poland—Warsaw—Biography—Juvenile literature. 4. Holocaust,
Jewish (1939–1945)—Poland—Warsaw—Juvenile literature. 5. Warsaw
(Poland)—Biography—Juvenile literature. [1. Korczak, Janusz,
1878–1942. 2. Jews—Poland—Biography. 3. Educators. 4. Jews—
Poland—Warsaw—Persecution. 5. Holocaust, Jewish (1939–1945)—
Poland—Warsaw.] I. Title. II. Series.
DS135.P63K573 1988
943.8'4—dc19   88-16138
[B]   CIP
[92]   AC

Published in the United States
by E. P. Dutton, New York, N.Y.,
a division of NAL Penguin Inc.

Published simultaneously in Canada
by Fitzhenry & Whiteside Limited, Toronto

Editor: Virginia Buckley

Printed in the U.S.A.   First Edition
10 9 8 7 6 5 4 3 2 1

to Erica and Nina
and to the memory of my father
(1905–1985)

Contents

Acknowledgments

Many people aided in the writing of this book, and I would like to thank them all.

I first heard about Dr. Korczak while I was teaching on a Fulbright exchange in Dijon, France, in 1978. One day I read in the newspaper that an elderly and semiblind Polish refugee, Benjamin Rozenberg, was attempting to organize a local commemoration to mark the centennial of Korczak's birth (1878). The description of the doctor and his career intrigued me. I arranged to meet Mr. Rozenberg and found that he needed help in his activities. A friendship resulted; I learned much about the German occupation of Dijon and the postwar years from this man who had lived through the persecution hidden in a tuberculosis sanitarium, and was in fact the sole survivor of a huge family that had been wiped out in Poland. He gave me copies of documents that he had found after the war, which detailed, person for person, the deportation of many Jews from the Burgundy region. In them I found families who may well have been my relations, and I discovered that I was living just across the street from the school yard that had served as the roundup point for these brutal actions. In fact, my daughter was attending nursery school there every day! The thought was chilling.

Knowing little about the Holocaust at that point, I resolved to look more deeply into Korczak's career when I returned to the United States, and used Mr. Rozenberg's own writings as an excellent introduction to help me begin serious research. We maintained contact for several years, and then there was silence. In the meantime I had begun to gather materials in English and wrote a few reviews of Korczak's work. Only after the manuscript for this work was well under way, and the decision made to write it for children, did a colleague from the Miami University French Department, James Creech, bring back the news from Dijon that Mr. Rozenberg had died a few years before. But he is still remembered fondly in his neighborhood and in this book, written in gratitude for his fine example of courage and commitment to social betterment.

Throughout, I had great help in my research from William Wortman, Sarah Barr, Kathleen Carels, and others on the Miami University Library staff who were eager to obtain interlibrary materials and track down sources. The university also supported my work with funds to purchase pictures, released time from teaching, and money for travel. Our English Department secretaries—Kathy Fox, Jackie Kearns, Virginia Tobeson, and Trudi Nixon—provided steady and intelligent help at every stage of the manuscript. Professor Kent Honeycutt of Indiana University supplied information on the Korczak asteroid.

The Lucius Littauer Foundation in New York awarded a generous grant in support of the book at a particularly critical time. Other helpful organizations included the Federation of Polish Jews, who sent a key article; the

Brigham Young University Library; and the Ghetto Fighters' Kibbutz in Israel. The archivist there, Mr. Reuven Yatsiv, was extremely helpful with photographic resources and correspondence.

The Polish Embassy in Washington sent several books from Poland on Korczak, and put me in touch with the Korczak Association in Warsaw, who were very encouraging. I have had a full and useful correspondence with Professor Erich Dauzenroth of the Korczak Archives at the University of Giessen in West Germany, which has kept me aware of recent developments in Korczak scholarship.

Dr. Phillip Veerman in Israel, a specialist on child welfare, has been of constant assistance by sharing his own writings and helping with Israeli contacts. He wisely suggested I write to Joseph Steinhart, who lived at Korczak's orphanage as a child. From Florida, Mr. Steinhart sent me a steady stream of personal recollections, family history, and even drawings of his youth in Warsaw. I have quoted from his own translation of Korczak's last march, which originally appeared in Emanuel Ringelblum's *Notes from the Warsaw Ghetto* and has since been reprinted in many histories of the war.

Dr. W. Lewin of the Korczak Medical Society in Kew Gardens, New York, has also done a great deal for the book. He too has vivid memories of Korczak, and established correspondence between me and other people, including Gershon Mandelblatt, who lived at the orphanage, and Mrs. Mary Marley, a relative of Stefa Wilczynska, Korczak's faithful comrade. His help and their responses have been invaluable.

The artist Israel Bernbaum has shared with me his unique pictorial impressions of Korczak and the children, and for their kind correspondence I am also grateful to Mrs. Leah Indelman, Marian Musgrave, Sidney Sulkin, Joe Hyams, Edward Kulawiec, Janina Bauman, and Kurt Bomze. I had help with Polish phrasing from Adam Mazur and Kazik Alster, and key encouragement when needed the most from my editor, Virginia Buckley.

At a vital time in the writing process, I was able to attend and address an international colloquium organized by the Swiss Korczak Association. The head of the group, Mr. Vladimir Halpérin, merits special gratitude for his warm enthusiasm in making certain I had ample meetings with people who had known life in the orphanages or had European sources of information on Korczak. I am grateful for their wisdom to Aleksander Lewin, Alicja Szlazakowa, Joseph Balcorak, Erna Mileva, and Ryszard Wasita; to the Israeli scholars from the Korczak Archives; and to Daniela Guzmán for her careful arrangements of my stay in Geneva. Their efforts made mine seem light.

Because it is still not easy to write about Korczak in this country, my book obviously owes much to all these scholars and friends—and to the unerring judgment and élan of my wife.

Who Is Janusz Korczak?

Who is Janusz Korczak? That was my first question when a call from my publisher notified me that *Bridge to Terabithia* had been nominated for the Janusz Korczak medal given biennially by the Polish branch of the International Board on Books for Young People.

Who is Janusz Korczak? Who is this man who is memorialized both in modern Poland and in the State of Israel? What has he accomplished that would inspire honor from Jews, Christians, and Communists?

On November 20, 1981, Patricia Allen, who was at that time publisher of Crowell Junior Books; Virginia Buckley, my editor; my husband; and I were invited to the Polish Embassy in Washington, D.C. There Ambassador Romuald Spasowski, the senior member of the Polish diplomatic corps, presented the Janusz Korczak Commemorative Medal to *Bridge to Terabithia*.

"I need to explain to you about this man," the ambassador said. And during the moving, informal ceremony in the embassy parlor, he talked of Korczak, who was one to the first physicians in Europe to devote his professional career to the nurture and development of children. He was also a director of two orphanages in the city of Warsaw—one Jewish, the other Gentile. Anti-Semitism eventually forced his resignation from the Gentile orphanage, and after the German invasion, he moved into the Warsaw Ghetto with his Jewish orphans. Friends offered to help him escape, but he chose to remain with his children. When they were taken to Treblinka, he went with them.

"I cannot claim," the ambassador went on, "that my father and Dr. Korczak were friends, but my father, too, taught pedagogy at the University of Warsaw, so they were colleagues. And since my father also died violently during the occupation, I always think of them together."

In November 1981, Poland was in turmoil. There were food riots in Warsaw on the same day that I accepted the medal and our small group enjoyed a leisurely lunch with the ambassador and first secretary.

Less than a month later, on December 17, Ambassador Spasowski resigned his post and defected, in order, he said, "to show my solidarity with the Polish people." I suppose that awarding that medal, honoring a children's doctor and teacher, to a writer of a book for children was among his last official acts.

I'll never forget that day at the embassy. Nor will I forget the comment on it made by a friend of mine. "What other country do you know of," she asked, "that has for a hero someone who gave his life for children?"

We do not live in a country that currently honors those whose lives are spent in the service of children. Our society alternately pampers children and abuses them, but it does not take them seriously. We shrug when we learn that every meal served in the Pentagon costs the taxpayer $14.00 and then protest that school lunches at $1.20 per child are too expensive. Ours is not a world that thinks first of the health and welfare of its children. If it were, would nations continue to pollute the air or poison the waters or threaten the destruction of the earth itself for the sake of immediate financial gain or political ideology?

The Nazis killed Janusz Korczak, but they could not destroy the ideals he stood for. We can destroy the civilized world, and we shall unless we begin to care, unless we begin to take with utter seriousness the children whose lives have been entrusted to us.

There is a story, retold in this book, about Korczak when, as a special lecturer in pedagogy, he assembled his university students in an X-ray laboratory. He had brought with him a little boy who was obviously made nervous by the sight of strangers, the darkness of the room, and the huge fluoroscope machine in front of him. The assembled students watching the fluoroscope screen saw the violent beating of the child's heart. In a quiet voice the good doctor told the students that the next time they were about to strike out angrily at a child, they should remember this frightened child and his fluttering heart.

To come to know Janusz Korczak is to remember the hearts of the children for whom he lived and died—to remember all children. And if we care for children, we will care for the world that is their only home. Which is why I am grateful to Mark Bernheim for his thoughtful and moving answer to the question, Who is Janusz Korczak?

KATHERINE PATERSON

1

"It's Modern Times, Jozef"

Even in the darkest days of war, people can illuminate life through heroism and love. This is the story of one such person, a children's doctor and author who was world famous for the books he wrote and the modern methods he introduced as director of two orphanages in Warsaw, Poland, before World War II. At birth called Henryk Goldszmit, as a young man he took the more Polish-sounding name Janusz Korczak to show his loyalty to Poland and the distance he felt from the Jewish roots of the Goldszmit family.

He struggled against prejudice and became one of the best-known figures in Poland during the 1920s and '30s.

But suddenly, at the start of World War II, he and the orphans he cared for were caught up in the holocaust of the Nazi invasion of Poland. Although he never thought that his life as a modern citizen would end trapped inside a ghetto, this is precisely what happened. His lifelong efforts to build a decent and peaceful life for the orphans seemed reduced to rubble, he and the children to ashes.

Today, Korczak is revered as a hero by both Polish and Jewish groups, and his achievements in the cause of children's rights are universally praised. He faced his ultimate challenge in 1942, in the most desperate days of the war. He stood up to the violence that was engulfing the world and showed that one elderly doctor could resist, at least for a time, the strongest machine of destruction ever invented.

The unselfish heroism and love for children that filled his life have survived and proved the strongest weapons of all.

His story begins in a more peaceful time, summer 1879, in Warsaw, once the capital of a free Poland but then part of the Russian Empire. The Poles have been living, unhappily, under Russian rule for almost one hundred years.

Warsaw, with its large Jewish population, has become a very modern city. The Jews have been here for many centuries. In the early 1800s, three out of four Jews in the world lived on Polish land; their numbers have increased even given the harsh Russian laws. Many are now attempting to modernize and gain acceptance into Polish society by being less Jewish. In fact, the ideal throughout Europe is to be a Jew inside the home, but a German, a Frenchman, or a Pole outside.

But this process, called assimilation, has created resentment in many Polish Catholics. It also makes religious Jews still following the old ways wonder if there is any future for Jews in Poland when they see the young generation's new ways of dress, speech, and prayer.

One such modern family is the Goldszmits. They have become so assimilated that they hardly consider themselves Jews at all. They feel Polish through and through, even if just a generation or two before their ancestors

JANUSZ
KORCZAK
1878
1942

One of the many statues erected in Poland to honor
Korczak. The sculptor is Edward Piwowarski; the statue
was dedicated in 1964. *POLAND* MAGAZINE

spoke Yiddish and lived in almost exclusively Jewish villages.

Jozef Goldszmit is a wealthy lawyer who specializes in divorce cases and has written a new guide, which is used in Polish courts. His own father had been a country doctor, a rare occupation for a Jew in those days. He also wore modern clothes, was educated, and spoke German, a sign of great sophistication.

To show his social standing, the doctor gave his other children Christian-sounding names—Maria, Magdalena, Ludwig, Carol. When Jozef chose a wife, it was Cecylia Gebicka, also from a very modernized family. In their new home, only Polish was spoken, and the Jewish religion was entirely absent on a day-to-day basis.

One afternoon, after waiting for Halina the serving maid to finish clearing the silver-rimmed luncheon dishes, Cecylia Goldszmit brought up a subject that had been vexing her for months. Despite many urgings, her husband still had not registered the birth of their baby, born almost a year before. Certain papers had to be obtained, forms filed and kept for later use in the child's life. Without them, she feared her son would be handicapped in his social progress within the Russian system, and the family's position might suffer too. She was determined this time not to be put off.

"Jozef," she declared, brushing away a few crumbs that Halina had not seen on the richly embroidered tablecloth, "I know that you don't want to talk about this, but it's almost a year since Henryk was born and you still haven't gone to the census office. What are you waiting for?"

She lowered her voice after glancing around to be certain that Halina was not in the room and reached across the wide table to press her husband's hand. His reluctance to comply with the regulations seemed ridiculous to her. "Don't delay any longer, Jozef. What are you so afraid of? This is 1879, not the Middle Ages. It's modern times, Jozef; things have changed, for the Jews, for everybody. Let's not be out of step; why shouldn't we act like everyone else?"

As he listened, Jozef Goldszmit was bothered again that his wife seemed to have forgotten her family roots so easily. He knew that one of her grandfathers had remained an Orthodox Jew, traditional in every way, to the end of his life. Once, when this man drew the lucky number in a lottery, he didn't even inform his family because he wanted to stay the poor glazier he had always been, putting in panes of glass for wealthy noblemen.

In naming their son, Jozef and Cecylia had chosen a truly modern Polish one, Henryk, as the equivalent of Hersh, his grandfather's Jewish name. This compromise, as they saw it, seemed sufficient to show that they valued the past but belonged in the modern Polish world too. Their son could have a bright Polish future, they hoped.

Despite what his wife said about being modern, and what he usually felt too, Jozef couldn't forget that in Poland conditions often changed fast. He remembered learning at school that Poland was called God's playground because of all the ups—and mostly downs—in its history. As a sort of joke, Emperor Napoleon had even called the Poles the white Negroes of Europe, because they had been treated so badly by everybody. Since the 1790s there hadn't been a free Poland at all, for Gentile or Jew. It was a roller coaster of a country, and none of the unpredictable rulers had ever been friendly to the Jews. So how could his wife be so sure of herself?

Even though he was a well-established lawyer, Jozef thought that the less he had to do with the authorities and the fewer records he provided them, the better. But he felt foolish trying to convince her of this when he wasn't sure of it himself.

He threw down the heavy cloth napkin in frustration. The cut glassware shook as his voice thundered, "What do you mean, 'afraid'? I just haven't gotten around to going to the registry office yet, that's all. I don't want to talk about it anymore. And it certainly won't hurt our friends the Russians not to know there's one more Jewish baby born in Poland. I'm in no rush to tell them."

Cecylia flushed. She was about to object angrily when Halina reentered carrying a lemon ice on Mrs. Goldszmit's newest acquisition. Instead she exclaimed, "Jozef, look at this gorgeous platter I bought the other day!" She went on about its value for some time and how she'd found it in an obscure antique shop, not noticing that his thoughts were elsewhere.

As he nodded absently, Jozef pondered the peculiar inheritance his baby had gained from these two families. Pious Jews to nonbelievers in two generations. The glazier had been married as a teenager to another orphan like himself, and in the town cemetery. It was a common superstition: When an epidemic broke out, the town elders thought a wedding in a cemetery would be good luck and stop the spread of the disease.

How life had changed! After-dinner ices on rare silver platters. Little Henryk lying on embroidered sheets in a carved cradle probably made for a Christian nobleman's baby. Taken for strolls in elegant parks Jews hadn't been able to enter not so long ago . . .

His thoughts continued to trouble him. He pondered why, with all these fine new ways, why cling to the past at all? Why not take the final and inevitable step—why not convert to Christianity and be done with all the indecision? Life would be so much easier. He knew many other lawyers who had done this; you could advance far more easily in the Russian system after you were baptized. It wasn't difficult to do these days. No one could prevent you, and no one in their families would object.

He had often imagined seeing a priest and beginning the process of joining the Polish majority. The future for

Henryk would be much easier; it seemed such a natural step.

But still, something held Jozef back. He felt at a crossroads; if they went in this direction, no return to being Jewish would be possible. His usual confidence was shaken when he thought of abandoning the old ways altogether. Even if he hardly practiced them, he knew them and they mattered to him a great deal. Unlike legal questions, which he could always solve rapidly, this matter of conversion was a problem without an answer.

As he worried over the problem of defining his family's religious identity, Jozef was aware that they were already living like Poles in almost every way. Their home was located in an elegant new part of the city where few Jews lived and was a showplace of everything that was fashionable.

Cecylia was clearly in charge. She appreciated luxury. A maid assisted her, brushing her long black hair a hundred strokes each evening and caring for her elaborate wardrobe and furnishings. She was proud of her social reputation; as the wife of a prominent attorney, she entertained frequently. Their modern home was the centerpiece of their existence.

Servants helped care for the crystal, the dark polished wood of the grand piano, the brocades, and the carvings. Knickknacks, imported rugs, and draperies were purchased and maintained under her careful supervision. She often remarked that it wasn't easy to keep up such standards. Both Henryk and Anna, his younger sister, were brought up mostly by the governess.

In this busy setting, it was easy to sidestep the nagging question of religion. Jozef Goldszmit hoped that in time such matters would disappear altogether. In a few generations his family had moved into real social acceptance. If things continued in this way, all distinctions separating Jews from other Poles would be gone. Perhaps they would never have to convert at all.

But when he was completely frank with himself, he had to admit that there could still be problems. Cecylia didn't seem aware, but things had to be handled carefully. It wasn't exactly true that he had forgotten to register Henryk's birth. He had deliberately put it off even though as a lawyer he knew what had to be done. He was worried about the future of the Jews. The Russians sometimes took young men, especially Jews, and kept them in the army for twenty-five years. This was part of their plan for the disappearance of Judaism. They intended to rule Poland forever, and they preferred a country without Jews at all, assimilated or not. Frequently, the men never returned, or if they did, they were completely Russianized and strangers to their families. Why be in a hurry to add Henryk's name to their list?

Jozef had a feeling that it would be better to risk possible confusion later in Henryk's life than to comply with the rule to register births immediately. In the official list of the Jewish community, the boy was recorded as Zvi Hersh ben Jozef (the son of Jozef). Let the Russians wait to learn about Henryk Goldszmit a bit longer.

2

A Proper Christian Funeral

As Henryk grew up, he had to face the choice of being Jewish or Polish. The first time he did so, at a very young age, he learned a lesson in prejudice and rejection so painful that even as an adult he always remembered it. For him, it was the beginning of a terrible loneliness he never escaped.

Being Jewish for him meant being alone. He didn't have the playmates he wanted. His mother seemed to disapprove of everything he wanted to do. *No* was her most frequent word.

One day he heard her cry with disappointment to his father after Henryk had refused again to play with Antony, a boy he hated, but of whose family she approved. They had recently converted to Catholicism, and she envied their social position. She instructed Nanny to be sure that Henryk and Antony played together in the park that morning.

"Watch out, Luisa, that Henryk doesn't embarrass us

again today. For some reason he doesn't seem to like Antony. I don't know why. I'm sure Antony didn't mean to rip Henryk's new kite, and anyway, his mother insisted she'd buy us a new one. As if I'd let her."

But that morning in the park was another disaster. Antony wore the red velvet suit that made Henryk think of dried blood. His close-set eyes were like a pig's, his fingers wet with drool. Henryk wanted nothing to do with this strong, fat boy. Why, he wondered, is Mama always making us be together? I hate him. I want to be with those children I can see from the window in my room, playing down in the courtyard—the janitor's son and all his friends. They have fun all day; they don't sniffle and whine like Antony.

When Luisa reported to Mrs. Goldszmit that this time Antony poked a hole in Henryk's new balloon and that their play had turned to bickering and tears, Cecylia went to her husband.

"Jozef, what are we going to do about Henryk? I've tried to get him to play with the right sort of children, but all he wants to do is sit and watch from the window what the ruffians in the courtyard are up to, and it's always something bad."

"Cecylia, I don't want to hear any more of this," Jozef said. "I myself wouldn't want much to do with some of your friends. The boy just sees things his own way."

"But Jozef, what a way that is! He's such a dreamer, and he fusses so over the smallest things. He takes everything to heart. I won't let him play with the wrong kind of children; there's no telling what he might pick up from them. Their parents pay as much attention to them as if they were orphans. They practically are."

Hearing these words outside the study door, Henryk wondered what it meant to be an orphan. Did it mean they hadn't any toys? He didn't care because he had too many, and he'd be glad to give them some if they wanted.

As long as he could be allowed to go downstairs and play!

Every day he saw the children down there running around and having fun while he sat alone in his room. They skinned their knees climbing the big chestnut tree in the center of the courtyard. They slurped water from a tap that he was sure his mother would say was filthy. They ate delicious-looking penny candies. One boy pushed a broom, others shoveled snow in winter, but always they sang loud songs for everyone to hear. Even in their fights they had fun, saying rude words that Henryk knew were not proper but that amused them greatly. He could just see into the shabby kitchen of the janitor's flat, but it looked much cozier than his own big apartment where nothing could ever be touched.

More than anything Henryk wanted to be a part of this happy scene. But his mother had strictly forbidden it. He'd show her. From here on, he'd refuse to have anything to do with Antony or other boys in the park where Luisa took him. He would stay in his room and take care of his pets. They were his only real friends.

At this time, when he was about six, he particularly loved Stashi, a tiny canary. All day he would watch the bird in its cage overlooking the broad avenue outside. He fed Stashi with table crumbs and pretended they could talk to each other.

Then one morning he found Stashi dead. Henryk wondered what to do. He knew you were supposed to do something, because he remembered Luisa telling him so when he had seen a long procession from his window. She explained that it wasn't a parade—it was a proper Christian funeral, and she moved her hand across the front of her uniform in a funny way when the wagon passed in front of them. He saw the flowers, the crucifixes, heard the singing, and knew that the dead person was going to be put into the ground in a special place.

But what about Stashi? Henryk didn't know any special songs or the things to say or do, but he knew that he had loved Stashi and he should do something. While his parents slept late, he confided his secret plan to the kitchen maid.

"I'm going downstairs to the courtyard and bury my bird in this old candy box, but don't tell Mama when she gets up or she'll be angry. I'll put some flowers over the box, too, and I'll make a big cross, like I saw."

The maid backed away from the box and shook her finger disapprovingly. "No, you mustn't do that. You mustn't, or I'll have to tell. That isn't right for you people to do, and you'll only get me in trouble if your mama knows you told me. You've got to have a Christian soul, a proper soul, to have a cross, and that bird hasn't got a soul at all. Only a proper Christian person can have a Christian soul; not a bird. You mustn't even talk about a cross; no, no, that's a sin."

Now Henryk was confused and frightened, not just sad. Things were not so simple. Whom could he ask? In the courtyard he heard the janitor's son and his friends already at play. They didn't always say no to everything. Maybe they knew about a cross for his bird. Then Mama would see that they were really smart, and she wouldn't go on saying that they were not right for him to be with.

In his heart, Henryk felt sure that these orphans, as she called them, would be able to help. He could give each one an extra toy he had, and then they wouldn't be orphans anymore. He ran downstairs with the box and went up to the janitor's boy. After Henryk told him about the canary and what the kitchen maid had said, the older boy came right to the point:

"Yeah, she's right, and that canary is a Jew, just like you are, 'cause it lived with you. It's going to go to hell, like you, when you die. Not me, 'cause I'm a Catholic and I'm going to paradise. The priest says so. But that canary and you and your family, you'll all go to hell, where it's dark all the time."

"I won't. I won't. I'm afraid of the dark. I won't go there."

"Yes, you will; the priest says so. Unless . . . listen, you bring me lots of sweets from your kitchen, and don't you tell nobody I told you to. Then maybe you won't have to go to hell with all the other Jews."

Even as the famous adult Janusz Korczak, Henryk remembered this childhood incident. How it had hurt to hear for the first time the old stories of Jews being damned to darkness and hell. How it had always been us against them. As a small child he had no idea what these prejudices meant, but only that he felt alone and different when he wanted to feel a part of something. Wasn't there some way he could have fun like the others and not be so lonely?

3

The Gypsy's Sack

On that day, after the janitor's son raced back to his friends, Henryk fled to his room. Stashi was now forgotten. Later, puzzled and afraid, he got up his courage and told his father what had occurred. Henryk begged Jozef to tell him they were not going to go to a dark place forever. But despite his courtroom wisdom, Jozef found himself unable to argue away his son's fears.

Finally he shouted in frustration, "You see, Henryk, why your mother and I don't want you to have anything to do with those children. They put nonsense into your head because that's all they have in theirs. We told you, stay away from them; they are not right for you.

"Listen to me: We live in a modern country now, and nobody with any sense believes any of that old rubbish. We are all the same now, Pole and Jew together, our family and his. I forbid you to have anything more to do with him. Or you'll wind up like him, in spite of everything we're trying to do for you, nothing but a . . ."

Later, Henryk realized that his father hadn't wanted to call him a blockhead or a donkey, but he couldn't help it. Jozef was impulsive and emotional, used to having his way. He couldn't understand that other children could also have a great influence on his son. Only Henryk's grandmother was a quiet comfort. She would pass the boy sugared raisins and call him her "little philosopher— always dreaming, always thinking."

For the first ten years of Henryk's life, his father remained the dominant influence through his strong will and commanding personality. Yet something seemed missing. Most of the time, Henryk was sure his parents loved him, but still—only Grandmother seemed to understand.

He went to her when he wanted to talk. One day he confided something that he hoped might bring him closer to the children in the courtyard who still fascinated him. "Grandma, why couldn't everybody just give away all their money? We have enough of what we need, don't we? Whatever I really want to touch I can't, and those children don't have much of anything. Why can't we share?"

"Ah, my little thinker. You're too young to know, but that's the way the world is."

"But, Grandma, I don't like things this way. I want to change everything so we could all start out the same. We don't need all these things. If those children had some of my things, then maybe we could all be friends, me and the orphans. Say it's a good idea, say it is!"

Another time, his grandmother comforted him when he couldn't sleep for many nights. Henryk had been out with his mother to look at a new acquisition at the antique dealer's. On the way back, they found their path blocked by a gypsy mother and her child, hands outstretched. At first, Henryk's mother tried to get around them, but the gypsy woman was experienced in street ways and whisked her skirts to make them stop. She mumbled some strange whining words and from under her scarves thrust her sooty child in their way. Holding tightly to Henryk's hand, his mother pressed three coins into his hand and led him a step toward them.

"Here, drop these coins fast into that sack she's holding, but don't go any closer, Henryk. These gypsies are all over the streets; goodness knows whose child that is she's gotten hold of. Probably not her own. Just using the poor thing to get some money. Here, give her the coins, that's right, and now we'll just go about our way."

"But, Mama, what if she follows and asks for more?"

"No, Henryk, three coins are enough, no more. If you let them think you have more, they might grab you and carry you off to the river in that sack. Next time we come here we'll take a different way."

Henryk unfortunately believed his mother too much. The image of the gypsies appeared in his dreams every night that week, and his grandmother had to stay with him to soothe him back to sleep. He couldn't get the picture of the woman opening and closing the sack out of his mind. Then, just when he began to forget the sound of her voice, another beggar came to the house, this time to the kitchen, where he had always felt safest.

In his *Ghetto Diary*, written when he was past sixty, he still remembered:

Beginning at Christmas, unemployed workers used to go from courtyard to courtyard in the richer quarters and, when summoned inside, present a show. A wooden box for a stage, an accordion, puppets for characters. The show was in the kitchen, so as not to carry in mud from the street. Cook put away small items because they stole. One time, two silver spoons disappeared. Then at the end, an old man with a bag took a collection. Shivering with excitement, I dropped the coins into his bag. But the man shook his long white beard and said, "So little, so little, my young master? Give us a little more."

One Christmas soon after, Jozef took his son to a famous Nativity drama at an orphanage on Freta Street. It was a kind of holiday ritual for wealthy children, but something very new to Henryk. He had no idea what to expect. Jozef did not go into any details about the Christmas story. On the way, Henryk trembled with anticipation. For some reason, he was sure the bearded beggar from the kitchen would be there too. Jozef thought he was cold and held him all the tighter, though Henryk only wanted to go home.

When they arrived at the crowded hall, a strangely costumed woman made the children sit in the first rows, far from their parents and very close to the stage. Henryk had no idea what was being acted out, and became overheated and nervous. When one of the old characters appeared holding a sack, it all became too much for him.

Jozef had to calm his son's sobs as they returned home. Though it was winter, he bought ices and sweets. He wrapped Henryk in his cloak, not noticing that the boy was damp with excitement. The next day Henryk fell ill; Jozef nursed him through several long nights of fever. He recalled how he too had suffered such nervous attacks as a young boy.

In time Henryk recovered. But he never forgot the terrors he felt whenever faced with beggars and open sacks. He feared that no matter how much he was able to give, even of himself, it would never be enough. There were so many who needed, and he was just one boy.

4

"Something Has Snapped"

Henryk was by now eleven, and life in the Goldszmit home continued much the same. New things to see and play with, to eat and wear; frequent glittering parties and many new faces. But lately there were also long periods of quiet when his father seemed strange and silent, his face gray, his eyes always down as if he were afraid. These times Henryk knew Jozef stayed home and secluded rather than go to his big offices in town. But why?

He knew only that Papa was very tired, worn out, as he heard Mama tell her friends. Then, after a time, the excitement would start again. He had heard his mother tell his father to take things a bit easier and "don't exaggerate so, Jozef," but in fact it was more fun when Jozef did act a bit wild. Wonderful games and sweets he would bring them, with no reasons.

One day in 1889, Henryk was surprised to see several serious-looking men—they all carried bags like Dr. Toma-siewicz so they must be doctors too—enter the apartment

Henryk as a young boy POLISH
KORCZAK ASSOCIATION

and go into the sitting room with his mother. She looked very different, with red blotches spoiling her usually elegant complexion. One doctor spoke softly and patted her shoulder.

"Now, Mrs. Goldszmit, in time he may come back to himself. But for now, something has snapped in his nerves, and he's really best left alone in quiet. Considering his profession, he surely should not see any clients for a time. Keep everything here as quiet as you can. Later, well, he may come back to normal."

The next weeks were one long hush. You tiptoed instead of walking. You stayed out of sight and hearing. Doctors came and went, and other visitors, maybe from the office, all looking worried and surprised.

But nobody told you anything, as if you weren't there.

Only in the kitchen did Henryk get some idea of what had happened.

One morning he heard Halina muttering about the master's breakdown, but she wouldn't say what that meant. She stopped when she saw the frightened look on Henryk's face. "Now don't you worry. Don't pay attention to what the doctors say. Halina knows, your daddy'll get better soon. Here, take this roll and butter and go play. . . ."

But Henryk had sensed danger in her confusion. Would Papa get better or not? What did a breakdown mean?

He resolved to listen for more information. It came soon enough. The next day he saw his mother's shock as she received from her cousin the full story of Jozef's collapse in the courtroom.

"No, Zelina, it can't be. He said that right in front of the judge? What did he think people would take him for? They must understand something came over him."

Henryk, too, couldn't imagine his father suddenly stopping in the midst of a confident examination of his own client. His arms thrown madly in front of his face, his body bent to the ground, Jozef cried in a choked voice, "They're here, they've come after me; go away. That's not my witness in the box, it's a devil come to mock me. Send him away, away."

What happened after, no one could say precisely. Somehow Jozef was taken from the court and brought home. He would look no one in the eye. For days he remained hidden in a corner of his room.

After a time, Henryk was allowed into the bedroom where his father lay in a dark calm. In the shadows Henryk could barely make out the pale face, but the haunted eyes were easy to see.

What Jozef said that day made no sense. This shadow wasn't the strong father Henryk had always known. Remembering Halina's words, he wondered how long his condition would last.

"Henryk," his father murmured, "listen to me carefully. I may be sick now, but I can see some things I wouldn't admit for a long time. I must warn you: Be on your guard always. Life is war and you never know when the real battle is going to start. Many people want to hurt us. Sometimes they only laugh and if you laugh back, they'll go away. But there are much worse ones. They are really dangerous; they aren't content with making fun, no—they want to hurt."

"Please, Jozef, no more," his mother interrupted and began to pull Henryk from the room. "Your father is still not himself, saying all these terrible things."

"No, wait, it's true," Jozef went on. "We are in a struggle all the time against those who think we are weaklings. They are evil; they only want to hurt those who do good. And this is the worst: They rule the world. They make the laws for their good, not ours. I found them in the courts, in the police and the government, everywhere. They've beaten me, Henryk. I can't fight them any more."

Jozef reached out to grasp Henryk's hand but fell back exhausted. Henryk was not sorry to leave the room. How could he fight enemies he didn't know existed? What was this battle he was supposed to be in? His father's condition frightened Henryk a great deal, but he was even more afraid of these attackers whom he couldn't see but who must be very strong to have made Jozef fall apart like this.

After one or two other such visits, Henryk had to admit he wasn't eager to see his father again. He felt an overpowering fear in the room. Although he still didn't know who these enemies were, he began to think that one day they might come after him too. He felt safer asking about his father's condition from afar.

Although he waited, things didn't improve. Then the family was told Papa couldn't get the kind of rest he need-

ed at home, and it would be better for him to go to a hospital for other people with his sickness. A permanent quiet
settled on the flat. Henryk never even saw Jozef leave.

Now no more parties, no spur-of-the-moment excur-
sions. Everything was dark and quiet. Henryk's mother
was a different person; she dressed plainly and brought
home no more new treasures.

After a few weeks, Jozef returned, still unwell. He
stayed in darkness and the doctors prescribed a more
permanent treatment. He left unseen again. Months went
by, but life did not resume its former style. Henryk had
to leave his private school, and the family moved to a
smaller place, because of "your father's sickness, you
know."

Great changes occurred that year for them all. After a
time they could not keep up appearances any longer.
Cecylia had to give up most of her possessions to be sold,
and the rest were moved into a small apartment in an old
section of Warsaw.

A new pattern of life emerged. Cecylia stayed in, avoid-
ing her former acquaintances and the parts of the city
where she feared she might see her favorite tea service
for sale in a shop window. Her delight in once buying
possessions now turned to bitterness, and she found no
pleasure in the few items she had been able to save. Her
room-sized rugs, her furs and jewels—all gone to pay for
Jozef's treatments.

He never returned to Warsaw alive. At the last asylum
he had to be tied down. Henryk grew up fast, realizing
that conditions would never be the same again. He knew
that his father's illness was something beyond the present
powers of medicine to cure, but mightn't others who fell
ill in such a way have hope? His grades were still excellent
at school, and he resolved to concentrate even more on
his studies, for through them he now had a goal in mind.

This decision—to study medicine—was something he

had been thinking about for some time. Not long before his father's collapse, his mother had found some poems that Henryk had written secretly. She showed them to Jozef, who was both amused and upset. Both parents knew that their son had a great love for reading and writing, but they were concerned where this would lead him.

"Henryk, be sensible," Jozef had urged. "Consider the life of a writer. So poor, such a struggle to get people to look at what you have slaved over. Think of it: With our family's connections, you could follow in your grandfather's footsteps and be a doctor. Now that's a real profession for someone with a mind like yours. Wouldn't we be proud of that, Cecylia?"

For once there was complete agreement between his parents. In his own mind Henryk, too, could see himself as a country doctor, calling on peasants and making their lives easier. Maybe he could write in his spare time. The idea immediately appealed to him. It was at this critical point in his life that the devotion to healing began. Jozef's death only made it stronger. Although nothing could be done for him, others could be helped.

When, a few years later, he sat as an eighteen-year-old in the Great Synagogue during his father's funeral services, much of what went on around him was incomprehensible to Henryk. He knew no Hebrew and couldn't follow the prayers. He got up and sat down when he saw the others do it. And all the while, the promise he had made kept going through his mind. He would carry on the family tradition and study medicine, and perhaps one day might be able to help people who were suffering as much as Jozef had.

Besides, he already understood that money was going to be a real problem for them. With what he could earn as a doctor, what better way was there to ensure that his mother and sister would never want for anything?

5

Rich and Poor

"I was rich. Then I was poor. I knew how it felt to have everything that could be bought, and then, to stare hungrily at others buying. I experienced it all; I saw things from all sides." So Korczak wrote later about the abrupt change in his family's condition following the disappearance of his father from their lives.

Sheltered as he may have been by his mother's efforts to have him mix with only the right children, Henryk at eleven was actually well-prepared for the new life that was thrust on him. He had never seen himself as she wanted him to be. Because he was always more interested in the have-nots, when he found himself one, he missed things less, never having cared for them to begin with.

"I was rich. Then I was poor. I lived both ways." He could remember how different his life had been that first winter in the cramped flat. No more surprise gifts from Jozef, little boxes left on a pillow or dinner plate and opened to disclose a shimmering brooch for Cecylia, a tiny doll carved from a nutshell for Anna, colored inks and crayons for him. No more bananas or pineapples to set mouths watering in the long Warsaw winters when tropical fruits were the greatest luxury.

Now his mother had to find ways to make things go further. Familiar faces were no longer seen. Only Henryk, his mother, and his sister—three survivors of the wreck of their comfortable past.

Henryk knew that now it was up to him to keep things going. Without being told, he sensed that responsibility had come to rest on him, just as he was becoming a man. To others he may have seemed pampered and lost in dreams, but he had real determination. He was glad to be rid of the many possessions that separated him from others who had little or nothing.

Now that his protected life was over, Henryk felt himself nearer to others, as he wanted to be. His thoughts often returned to the noise and clamor of the funeral. In the huge synagogue, where he had never set foot before, he had been amazed to see throngs of Jews—men dressed in prayer shawls, women strictly apart from the men and crying loudly—surrounding him and his family as if they belonged there.

And the words the rabbi had spoken remained alive to Henryk: "The Jew more than any other man realizes himself within his national community. As a Jew he can exist only insofar as he belongs to it."

Henryk was puzzled because he couldn't see how this applied to them. Jozef had little to do with this community of Jews before he became sick, at least as far as Henryk knew. Why had they come to mourn him now?

It was true, he remembered hearing about a series of books his father had written before he was born, on divorce in Jewish law and some biographical sketches of

famous modern Jews. Jozef's brother Jakub had also written articles for Jewish magazines. But in his own lifetime
Henryk had seen nothing of religious belief from either of
his parents. He thought Jozef intended them to be fully
Polish, so what did the rabbi's words mean?

Where was this national community? Poland? Russia?
Somewhere else? Could the Jews belong to any country
the same as non-Jews did and yet remain Jews, with this
extra ingredient? Was it possible? Was this why the others
always resented them?

Henryk knew that Jozef had taken real pride in having
them be like the Poles. Little had separated him from the
lives of his schoolmates. If Jozef had not suffered a
nervous collapse, they might still belong to this Polish
community, not the Jewish one.

It was a riddle to him. He knew nothing about a
national community of Jews. How could he feel a part of
it? The rabbi surely knew that they never came here to
pray. Had he said that because he thought not being a
part of the community had led to Jozef's breakdown? Had
it?

Only one thing seemed clear to Henryk: He was going
to find a new identity for himself and his family. The
people his parents had been so proud to entertain, especially his mother—where were they now? They didn't
seem to need the Goldszmits at all. In fact, Henryk
recalled how often his mother had been furious when
someone she was pursuing snubbed her socially. The
smallest thing could be seen as an insult, and often was.
Well, from here on, he would find different people,
whether they were Jews or not.

There were people who needed things done for them,
who needed to be taught or given assistance. Henryk was
sure he could find this community for himself and his
family right here in Poland. With his writing and his

studies he knew he could accomplish important things and make people need him as much as he needed them.

Henryk learned something else in his new existence, too. He came to see that, no matter what group he decided he belonged to, he was going to have to deal with two basic types of people. There was no getting away from the constant struggle between them, the weak against the strong. The strong didn't seem to need anyone else. They were in charge of things and took what they wanted. They had money and lived the way the Goldszmits used to; they wanted only to be with others like themselves.

Then there were the weaklings. They depended on the strong; they gave, often against their will. At school, the tough boys took their things and bossed them right from the start. Fights broke out when the weak ones forgot their place, but the results were always the same.

The struggle for power went on everywhere. More than once Henryk came home from school with bruises on his face or clothes ripped at the knee. He couldn't stand by and watch someone get pushed around; he longed to set things right. In his community there would be no such cruelties.

Yet in his present life the taunts rang in his head until they were as familiar as daily lessons. Usually they were the crudest kinds of insults to Jews, curses based on tales heard at home or at church. Henryk had no answers to them. How could he spread love when hate seemed so strong? How could the weak be made strong?

One day he returned home more upset than usual. At first he wouldn't tell his mother, but later the whole story emerged as she washed the bruises and he winced at the burning disinfectant she applied. This time the incident involved a boy Henryk didn't even know, an unfortunate who had wandered into the wrong street after school.

Immediately the bullies began pelting him with stones. When they saw he was an "onion-eating scabby jewboy" their fury increased, and they continued the punishment beyond its normal limits for someone who dared enter their territory from another street.

"Oy, oy, where's your rabbi? Who will help you? Oy, oy, who will help you?" they hooted and threw rocks until the boy fell to his knees while the stones continued to bounce off him.

Henryk had stood rooted to the spot at first, silently urging the boy to run away while he could. The few passersby paid no attention, having witnessed such scenes many times before. When Henryk couldn't stand it anymore, he rushed into the middle of the street and frantically pulled the smaller boy, now stunned beyond caring, to his feet.

"Hurry, get out of here, fast. Just get out; run down that alley there. It'll take you into the next street, and then look for the policeman who stands by the bank. He probably won't help you, but if these boys follow you down the alley and see him, they'll probably stop."

By now the rocks were hurting Henryk too. Just then one hit him hard right under the eye, and he felt something warm and sticky run down his face. His cheek began to hurt terribly. The bigger boys began to yell at him too, and he heard them cry, "Let's get both them Jews. We'll teach them."

Henryk dragged the smaller boy to his feet with a sudden burst of strength. He pushed him along ahead of himself down the alley. Without saying a word, they separated when they saw light again, and each ran off in the direction of safety.

Although he hadn't actually fought back directly this time, Henryk felt glad he had done something to stop the attack. "If I hadn't run out there while they were throwing stones, Mama, he would have just lain there taking it; they saw how weak he was and they wouldn't have stopped. He was bleeding, Mama, so I had to do something, don't you see? Owww, that hurts; it stings when you do that."

All Henryk's frustrations poured from him along with his tears: "Why do they act like that, Mama? It isn't right. Why do they always pick on the little ones? And all those things they say about Jews. I wish I could talk to them and make them see we don't have to be enemies, but all they want to do is make fun and fight, and hurt.

"Where do they get those things they say about us? I don't think they even understand what they're saying; they just copy. I know I could be friends with them if they didn't have such stupid ideas. I know I could change the way they think if I had a chance."

At times like these, Cecylia wished Henryk's father or his grandmother were there to reason with him. How could she, confused and alone as she felt, calm his nerves or tell him what to do? Whatever answers he'd find, she feared he'd have to discover them on his own.

What Henryk did find was increasing evidence that his place had to be with the givers, not the takers. In the battle for survival, as a child he had been completely under the control of adults who ignored his rights and expected him to remain silent. As a family, the Goldszmits had lost their security with their regular income and were under the control of the wealthy who ruled society. And as Jews, even though Warsaw then had more Jews than any other city in Europe, they were in the weakest position of all, open to every form of prejudice with no real protection from the law.

Each of these conditions called out for change, but what could one boy accomplish? Henryk knew only that he would have to keep fighting and apply all his strength as he had decided at his father's funeral. When you were as liable as they were to be pushed around, you had to be strong and keep your dreams clear in your mind.

Into his teenage years, he tried his best to make his family's life more bearable. Often he and his sister went for long walks when they sensed their mother would rather be left alone. They had to pass the fashionable area where they used to live, each silent in thoughts of the past.

One gray afternoon, just as they were about to retrace their steps and return home for dinner, they saw a familiar object in the shop where their mother had brought many of her prized possessions when they had to move.

"Anna, isn't that the tablecloth Mama used to have in the dining room? Don't you remember it? I think that's it, I really do. Anna, don't you remember how she would spread it out on the table with all the crystal and silver on it?"

But Anna needed no prompting to see the picture again in her mind. She, too, could envision the gold and deep green velvet cloth; she could feel the raised embroidery of the fruits and leaves in the center. How often as a little girl she had traced with her finger the outline of the scrollwork in the border and marveled at the sheen of its surface reflected in the light of the chandelier.

Together brother and sister stood for a few moments in a common shame. Henryk had often spoken to Anna of how little he cared for the luxuries of their past, but now it hurt to see this reminder of their parents' pride displayed for sale openly in a shop window. Henryk felt angry, at himself, at his father, at the owner of the store— at everyone.

"Anna, do you think we could buy it ourselves and give it to Mama for her birthday? Our table now isn't so grand, and we haven't got much to display on it, but maybe it would make her feel a bit better just to have it. Maybe we'd all feel better, Anna; it'd be like Papa coming home again with a surprise package. Oh, let's try to get it back."

Anna was as eager as Henryk, but the children had little chance of success. They hadn't an idea of what it cost and were too nervous to enter and ask. Every day for a few weeks they stopped in front of the window and stared at the tablecloth, thinking how lovely it would look if they had it again on their table.

Anna had saved a tiny sum of money, just a few coins, and Henryk himself had recently begun to give private lessons to younger boys whose mothers had heard about his high standing at school. Although he faithfully gave the small amounts to his mother, occasionally he would keep a little, though he hadn't known why. Now he did. Over the next few weeks, he gave extra lessons and carefully hoarded the change.

Then one afteroon he took the suede purse with his savings and hurried with Anna to the store. In truth, the amount they had could have bought only the cheapest napkin, but the two children had convinced themselves that the owner would sell them what they wanted. He had to.

Turning the corner and approaching the large window, they pressed each other's hands tightly. Henryk looked above the tea table where the tablecloth had hung, but where was it? In its place there was a dark-colored painting of a dead bird on a dull silver platter, surrounded by waxy-looking fruit. Ugly yellow feathers with brown dots, and apples that looked more like paving-stones— where was Mama's cloth? Where had the man moved it to just now when they had to come to take it home?

Without hesitating, Henryk pushed open the door and

rushed inside. A man wearing a shop apron turned around from rearranging the contents of a china cabinet and answered Henryk's question simply. That "leftover old cloth" had been thrown into the bargain of a recent sale: Somebody needed something to cover up a stain on an old couch.

"Too bad, sonny; I didn't know you were interested," was his sarcastic end to the conversation.

The children could console themselves as they trudged home only with the certainty that Mama had never known of their intended surprise. Fortunately they had never mentioned it to her, and she had developed the habit of averting her eyes from windows where she might see things she couldn't have. The next day, when Henryk presented her with a slightly larger sum from his earnings, her momentary pleasure was dimmed only by the realization that there was so much it would have to cover. Then she began figuring: This extra sum could surely be put to good use. Perhaps Henryk had the time to take on a few extra pupils every week.

6

Korczak

As he grew into a teenager with heavy responsibilities, Henryk dreamed of making important changes in the world. Although he had promised his father that he would devote himself to becoming a doctor, he had never really given up the hope that he would also be able to write about the injustices of life. To get ideas, he read all the time—late at night in his room, then again early each morning before his mother and sister were awake, even at the table, which earned him rebukes for his bad manners.

Like other boys his age, Henryk loved best to read adventure stories and imagine himself in combat against powerful enemies, but unlike most others he felt more involved with the victims than the heroes. The more hopeless the situation, the more he became the outcast or the injured one. He never saw himself as a fearless hero overcoming supernatural creatures in fantasies. He knew you didn't escape suffering that easily; you had to keep fighting for power against much stronger people.

Henryk seemed to be on the run continually. He rushed about the city keeping his appointments as a tutor. His mother had gotten him some jobs at first, and from those recommendations he got others. Parents were amazed at his patience, and soon he was teaching more children than he had time for. Everyone called him a born teacher for the way he helped even the dullest and laziest children. He got closer to many of them, especially the unhappy ones, than did their own parents.

More than the small sums of money he was able to give his mother, Henryk welcomed the possibility his tutoring gave him to see the life of Warsaw up close. The city was growing fast, with electricity and gas lines, trams, and wide new avenues being pushed through the crowded old sections. Factories drew young people looking for new lives away from the routine and poverty of the land.

In the hearts of Poles, hope grew that one day soon the Russians would tire of ruling their country and leave them to be free again. In Russia itself things were changing: Young educated people were demanding rights, and to Poles it seemed only a matter of time before their own nation would be reborn.

The Jews played a significant role in the growth of Warsaw. Their numbers increased steadily as the city became modernized. There was no real ghetto, an area where Jews had to live, as in the past, but in fact a large part of the city had become a thoroughly Jewish district. Most of the stores and many of the small industries were owned by Jews, and when Polish Christians tried to enter these trades there was friction and resentment. Although they made up a full one-third of the city's population—more than anywhere else in the world—Jews felt very insecure. Assimilation had brought those who were eager to change into close contact with the non-Jewish world, but the old prejudices were still there and often flared into violence.

One day when he had that rarest of all things, a few spare hours, Henryk sat in his favorite place in the city, the dark and cool Saxon Gardens, where even today lawns and flowers bloom. He was a familiar visitor to the park, among the vendors and nursemaids pushing the prams of the wealthy, as he had been pushed as a baby. Elderly folks, dressed warmly despite the heat outside, sat talking in small groups under the chestnut trees.

Henryk often engaged them in conversation, telling them about his strict mathematics teacher or reciting a few lines of poetry from the Polish national favorite, Adam Mickiewicz, or the great Russian writer Leo Tolstoy. Henryk especially admired Tolstoy because the great man had undergone a religious conversion and publicly devoted himself to the betterment of humanity. To his friends in the Saxon Gardens, Henryk was the young philosopher he had been to his grandmother years before. "So young and so serious . . . such a dreamer," they observed.

But today he was in the park to meet a special student he was helping with her lessons. This daughter of a wealthy family had a deep charm for him. She was quiet and refined, always dressed like a young noblewoman— curly gray fur on the collar of her maroon coat and matching hat in winter, or a perfectly pressed sailor dress on a warm day like today. Henryk loved her, as he loved the heroines of the adventure stories he read, more like a sister or a cousin in need of protection.

As he remembered his young passions fifty years later:

From seven to fourteen I was permanently in love, always with a different girl. There was a little tight-rope dancer; I grieved bitterly over her dangerous occupation. I loved for a week, a month; occasionally two at once, three. I had feelings that rocked and shook me. Then the world excited me, but now I have learned that I should exist not to be loved and admired, but to act and to love others. I am duty-bound to look after the world.

On this particular day Henryk waited in vain. Perhaps Katja was not well, or at the last moment her mama had taken her off to a more exciting afternoon downtown. Probably the appointment they had made to meet him meant little to them. Henryk had no way of knowing, for he had come directly to the gardens from another tutoring job and sat waiting, growing more forlorn as the shadows lengthened. Finally he left the park, barely nodding to his old friends sitting close together to gather the last afternoon warmth.

Henryk was determined to give his deep disappointment a literary voice. He wrote a poem about his heart's sadness:

> Ah. Let me die,
> Let me descend to my dark grave. . . .

He kept the poem in a secret place until one day he was taken on a visit to the editor of a well-known Sunday newspaper literary magazine. This man, Alexander Swietochowski, had a reputation for frankness, so Henryk had to summon up all his courage to recite his poem of heartbreak, ending with,

> Ah. Don't let me live,
> Let me die.

The editor thought silently for a few seconds, which to Henryk seemed longer than the whole time he had waited for Katja. When the editor finally spoke, he said only three words: "I'll let you."

Henryk wrote no more poems after that. Gradually his romantic feelings became mixed with religious ones, in which he imagined God as a stern opponent facing man. Without any religious training whatsoever, Henryk didn't have any real theories of creation or salvation. Instead he saw life as a kind of courtroom in which man and God spoke about important things. Man might ask God for something specific, and there was a chance he might get it, but no guarantee. Henryk hoped he might be able to make God a kind of ally in his fight for justice and reform. He knew this was hard to do, so he prayed often, "Please God, give me a hard life. Let it be very hard, but let it be full of aspirations and beauty too."

At seventeen, he tried writing his first novel. It described a young hero, like himself, obsessed with the fear of having inherited madness from his father. He called the book *Suicide,* and poured his heart into writing it.

The book was a kind of cure. He felt better for having put his deepest fears into words. Fighting off insanity and the temptation to suicide through hard work in a book and in his own life made him feel mature. He was ready to devote his time to both literature and medicine, because becoming a doctor would be his way of reaching and helping those who really needed him. As he wrote to a friend:

> What else is there left for me? After all, literature is only words, whereas medicine is deeds. I must earn a regular living. A writing career is too unsteady and teaching is out of the question because of all the Russian restrictions. I *must* be a doctor.

Having made the decision, Henryk applied to become one of the few Jewish students who could be accepted for medical studies at the University of Warsaw. A strict quota system was designed precisely to keep out the large

Henryk in the uniform of a university student

number of assimilated Jewish young men and women. Of course it also served to sharpen the bad feelings of competition between the Jewish and Christian Poles. The Russians knew very well that this antagonism could work for their benefit. They used the divide-and-conquer system as long as they ruled Poland.

Henryk's outstanding grades got him admitted. Before he was twenty, he began his studies full-time and took on even more tutoring jobs, rushing from one end of Warsaw to the other. He taught the children of the rich and not-so-rich. He kept at his university studies with a fanatical drive to achieve the highest grades and prove to his family that he was capable of taking care of them. He slept little, wandering the city streets until late at night.

At this time he became a close friend of an unusual young man, the rebellious poet and writer L. S. Licinski. Under his influence, Henryk set out to taste life on his own. Although continuing to support Anna and their mother, he went to live in an especially run-down section of the city. With the poverty-stricken Licinski as his guide to the underworld, Henryk made himself familiar with living conditions he had only imagined before.

There were neighborhoods that hadn't changed in ages except to become worse. Beggars and laborers lived side by side in squalor, without any sanitation or privacy. Orphans and abandoned children were left on their own, in conditions far worse than Henryk could recall from the courtyards of his own youth. Why, those children his mother had forbidden him to play with lived like kings compared to these. Here were boys and girls in tatters, catching on to the coats of every passerby to whine for food, or even alcohol for the older ones. These children had never seen the inside of a school, wore the same patched rags season after season, and, for a future, aspired to nothing more than crime and drunkenness.

Henryk was drawn to their misery like a moth to a flame. To do something about changing these conditions, he felt he had to live them first. As he told Licinski after one especially terrible night of wandering along the bridges by the evil-smelling river, where homeless adults and children slept under old newspapers, "I want to write of human minds, of misery and happiness; fights with evil against brotherhood and love—in short, the Tomorrow of Humanity."

Now he had another plan. He could combine writing about the appalling conditions of life with doing some-

thing about them through medical care. He could special-
ize in the treatment of children—pediatrics—to bring the
latest advances to those who needed them the most, the
future generations of Poland.

He had always been drawn to children in need and all
his life had tried to get closer to them. Now he could
learn practical ways of improving their health and at the
same time try to change the reasons which kept them so
poor. What better way to fight the weakness of his own
family's state, and the fear of insanity inherited from his
father, than to devote himself to being strong and building
a better world for the children?

It was at this time that Henryk also underwent a basic
change in his own identity. It happened that shortly
before he was twenty he heard about a literary competition under the sponsorship of the famous Polish pianist
Ignace Paderewski. Entrants were free to submit anything
they wished; Henryk had written a serious play about
mental illness called *Which Way?* that he hoped would
impress the judges. But he thought that as a young Jewish
medical student he might stand a better chance of winning
with a Polish-sounding name.

The day before the entries were due, and still puzzled
how to sign his play, he saw a book in the library by
Jozef Kraszewski, a well-known writer of adventure stories
and old-fashioned tales of Polish nobility. The book was
called *About Janasz Korczak and the Squire's Daughter;* Henryk
liked the hero's name and decided to borrow it for
himself, but he hadn't counted on a careless typesetter
switching one letter for another. When his play was
printed as having won an honorable mention prize, its
author was listed as *Janusz Korczak.*

The misspelled name stuck and gave Henryk an idea.
Winning in the contest represented more than just the
award—it gave him a new identity, as well as entry into

the world of recognized authors. In a sense, he could become a new person with two times the strength for the struggle ahead.

For the next forty years, he remained Dr. Henryk Goldszmit, an assimilated Jew who ran the day-to-day affairs of two orphanages for hundreds of children and served in four major wars. At the same time, he was also Janusz Korczak, a famous Polish writer, a hero, and an extraordinary man who fulfilled his childhood promise to make the world a better and more peaceful place. He truly seemed two men in one.

The children themselves simplified the question of who he really was. They most often called him Pan Doktor, an affectionate but respectful combination in Polish of *Doctor* and *Pan* (Mister) into one well-loved Mister Doctor, who stood between them and the problems of the world.

Unfortunately, he was not able to hold onto this ideal for long. The events of history swept it brutally aside. Although Henryk Goldszmit, the early Jewish self, seemed to fade comfortably into the background and become replaced by the more famous Korczak, when the Nazi invaders seized power in 1939, they lost no time in identifying him again as a Jew and an enemy marked for destruction. To them, the name Korczak was just a trick by a Jew trying to be somebody he was not. They put all people into rigid categories of the racially acceptable and the outcasts—no invented selves permitted, no make-believe double identities. Korczak was unreal, a childish pose that meant nothing to them, and was in fact a danger to their total control over every life.

But to Henryk, when he first used it, the name was of the greatest importance. It was very real. It was freedom. It was the chance to escape from the limitations of the past into a new person without barriers of race or religion. At twenty, all he hoped to achieve in life now seemed open to him.

7

Into the Slums

As the new century began, Henryk—now both author and medical student—passed into young adulthood. He made his name known at the university as among the most promising young doctors-to-be. Others envied his mind but were puzzled by the long hours spent in the worst slums of the city, working—for nothing—with the poorest families, trying to educate them in the fundamentals of care and sanitation and give them a sense of the importance of learning to read and write.

Using the name Korczak, he wrote many essays based on his experiences in the hovels along the broad Vistula River that flows through Warsaw on its way to the North Sea. Henryk seemed to find time for everything, burning his youth in long hours of activity with a minimum of sleep. Everything to Excess seemed to be his motto.

Once he went with his bohemian friend Licinski to a part of the city where prostitutes walked openly, and disease was rampant. Outside a disreputable tavern, the two men saw a pair of hoodlums circling each other with knives whose blades were throwing up sparks under the sickly yellow streetlight. Every imaginable curse dropped from their drunken lips. They spoke a gutter Polish that Henryk could barely understand, but even the coarse onlookers would gasp with horror at an especially wicked oath. First one thug, then the other leaped to wound with a lightning flash of the blade. Soon both men's faces were full of cuts and slashes. No one knew why the argument had started, or cared if it ended with the men dead or alive. This was a nightly occurrence.

Henryk and his friend stumbled into the middle of the duel. Licinski backed off quickly, but Henryk stood rooted to the spot in horror. The brawlers were not much older than he; they had probably grown up as abandoned children in this same neighborhood. Were the sickly prostitutes on the next street their sisters—or their mothers? To have survived in this environment for twenty years required a kind of intelligence of its own, and surely strength. Now in a senseless fight one or both would soon fall, perhaps fatally wounded. Whatever potential they had was about to be extinguished.

Suddenly Henryk rushed in between the men as they separated and prepared for a final assault. The crowd gasped in surprise. What a dangerous thing to do! Some of them recognized this small young man with the thinning red hair and warm smile; they knew him as the young doctor-student who had tried to teach the alphabet to some of the neighborhood kids.

"But what is he doing getting mixed up in this fight? He really must be crazy to interfere. Look, he's running up to one of them, the bloodier one, and putting his arms around him to help him get up. Now, he's kissing him on his filthy cheek. And now he's helping the other one and kissing him."

"Brothers, enough of this, enough. Put away your

knives. Stop hurting each other, enough," cried Henryk.

"Now, look—he's laughing and trying to get them to put away the knives. He'd better watch out, or somebody'll take a blade to him one day. Some brothers they are."

Another time Henryk returned home in the middle of the night after roaming with Licinski through the seediest parts of Warsaw. He overslept the next day and his mother had to come to his flat to wake him up. When she saw the condition of his muddy boots and torn clothes, she scolded him for not living up to the standards of a medical student. To tease her, he protested, pretending to be sleepier than he really was. He stretched and yawned loudly. "A doctor, Mother? Why, haven't you noticed me lately? I've been taking some new classes from different teachers. Now I'm studying to be a lush."

For such reasons, and from what she heard about other, similar incidents, Mrs. Goldszmit had come to disapprove of her son's ways and friends. What would they lead him to? But she needn't have worried, for Henryk himself soon felt that he had had enough of this type of life. He realized that Warsaw, although it was growing all the time, was removed from the really modern capitals of Europe. Actually, it was a wonder that it was as advanced as it had become; the Russians were so repressive.

No doubt one day they would be gone, back to their own country; then the Poles could take their place again among the free people of the world. For now, anyone who wanted a real education had to go abroad—Berlin, Vienna, Paris, London. Medical schools and doctors there were accustomed to eager young Poles seeking the freedom to study and learn for the profession. They returned to Poland with the new techniques they needed. Henryk knew that he too would have to take this path if he was going to succeed in his desire to be among the leaders of a reborn nation where every citizen could lead a healthy life. Having tasted a wild existence for a few years, he knew he would soon settle into a life devoted to learning and practice.

In the meantime, Henryk had to finish the last few years of medical school and also serve a training period in the Russian Imperial Army. Jozef's old fears of Henryk's disappearing forever into the wilds of Russia never materialized. As a medical student, Jew or not, Henryk was too useful to the Russians to be wasted like that. The Russian army had to stretch across many thousands of miles, and medical personnel were always desperately needed. The peasants were taken for service and used until they dropped. Doctors had to be there to keep the army going.

Henryk did not have to stay too long. He was permitted to return to Warsaw to complete his degree in 1903. He already had something of a reputation. Two years before, his first full-length novel had been published, but since the author was identified as Korczak, not many knew that he and the young army doctor were the same.

The book, *Children of the Street,* was about the lives of the street waifs and beggars he had met in the slums of the city in his student days. He had wished it to be published by the editor of a magazine he greatly admired, the weekly satirical review *Thorns.* As the name suggested, this was a magazine that wanted to stick its readers with sharp and biting comments. Naturally, the authorities and censors often did not approve.

This idea of creating stinging opinions appealed greatly to Henryk. He asked the editor, Alexander Pajewski, to print his novel to shake up the middle-class readers, but Pajewski had a better idea. Some other young writers had recently approached him. Each wished to bring his work to the attention of the public, but Pajewski's resources were limited.

Couldn't they combine their efforts into a kind of

cooperative effort? From this came the idea of a serialized book, each young man writing a part: The chapters would be strung together and the public could decide which it preferred.

This was a challenge that Henryk responded to well. He welcomed the idea of pooling his labors with others; some of the writers struggled to produce anything because they resented the arrangement, but Henryk came up with three full chapters. Pajewski gave the finished novel the catchy title, *Diary of a Mad Butler*. Everywhere those days talk of madness was in the air. Throughout the old empires of Europe, the young were protesting and urging reforms. Revolutions seemed likely, and educated young people were eager to lead the way. Few enjoyed being radical more than Henryk.

His three installments in the collective book appeared under the pen name Hen-Ryk. They were so well received by the public that Pajewski decided to take a chance and publish the full manuscript of *Children of the Street*. Although the total sales were not impressive, the fact of finally having brought these terrible conditions to the attention of the public was a tremendous incentive for Henryk to go on. Now he was glad he had written down so many observations on the backs of cigarette packs and other scraps of paper as he roamed the slums.

At this time, Henryk was also working in several Free Libraries organized by the Warsaw Charitable Association. In most countries then, facilities like libraries were not free, as they usually are today. They were sectarian, supported by a particular group, usually religious. The idea of a public reading place, where the common people would be welcome, was virtually unknown, just as orphanages, asylums, homes for the elderly, and other public institutions did not exist for everyone.

In addition, because religious identity in Poland was an

explosive issue—the Russians and Poles were not of the same Christian sect, and Jews were a very large minority—facilities had to be kept distinct among the different groups, and often were wastefully duplicated.

But these Free Libraries really were for everybody. They especially hoped to attract the poverty-stricken who had no other access whatsoever to books. Radical young Poles like Henryk were sure that the Russians preferred to keep the Polish masses illiterate. Like all rulers occupying a country, their chances for remaining in power were greater if the majority of the population did not advance socially and couldn't be reached by any revolutionary writings.

To the Russians, the Free Libraries could be a real menace. In fact, the organizers of the libraries did set up secret schools too. They had to be prepared to move at a moment's notice. They taught the poor for a few hours on a Saturday, packing and unpacking crates of cheaply printed pamphlets that served as teaching and reading materials. Often they were only a step or two ahead of the authorities.

Henryk was devoted to this activity in his final years as a medical student. He encouraged many of the slum dwellers he met in his wanderings to come to the libraries. Since many of them were unused to controlled behavior, the atmosphere often resembled the streets rather than a library. Henryk alone seemed able to control them. Having no experience with being in a school, the children and teenagers shouted and pushed one another, yelling jokes and insults and grabbing what they wished. When he was able to afford to serve them some sweets after the lessons, the crush to get the best morsels was a stampede. Everything was reduced to crumbs before the littlest ones had anything.

In whatever other free time he had from studying or tutoring, Henryk visited children in hospitals throughout the city. When children were ill enough to be taken to a hospital, all too often they never came back—or such were the fears among the uneducated. To them, the clang of the ambulance meant that all hope had been abandoned. For children taken to a charity ward in a large city hospital, they were sure that nothing could be done. No wonder they needed reassurance so much.

Henryk understood the fears of the children completely. A visit from him meant that somebody cared. When he heard that an epidemic had caused many children to be quarantined, he visited as many of them as he could, promising them that they would soon be back at play in familiar surroundings. Thanks to him, they could believe it was possible to get well in a hospital.

Often he would keep in contact with those who recovered and went home. In his own poor flat he entertained them with something called an epidiascope, a kind of magic lantern show. On a borrowed screen, colored pictures were projected. Henryk did the voices; the children roared with laughter when he pretended to chase them with the voice of the feared police or secret militia.

These days Henryk wore the blue uniform of the university, with a cap trimmed in silver braid. He never brushed or took care of his clothes, and so, like everything else he had, his cap looked worn, as he wanted it. To the slum children, he seemed as young as they were, one of them. But to the other medical students, he was still a puzzle. He was irresponsible and unprofessional because he didn't seem to care about a successful career as they did. They wondered how he was able to excel in his studies and still find the time to publish his sketches of slum life as well as be a familiar face in the charity wards and clinics for the poor.

8

The Young Doctor

In the early years of the twentieth century, all was growth and change in both Henryk's life and Polish society. Strong currents flowed under the surface of the strict Russian rule. Radical new ideas that were to lead before long to the Communist revolution in Russia were popular in Poland too. Talk of socialism and overthrowing the Czar was everywhere.

Young Jews were especially active in the fight for freedom and the rebirth of an independent Poland, as they were in Russia itself. The desire grew for human rights, and for liberation from the rule of the church, the army, and the monarchy that kept things as they had always been. Polish Christians and Jews alike were convinced that things would change soon.

Within the large Jewish population itself, many different voices were heard. Some urged religious revival to combat increasing assimilation. Others were against religion alto-

gether and wanted the Jews to fight as one nation of
workers for socialism.

Many others, including some who later became leaders
of Israel, were fervent Zionists urging Jews to move to
Palestine, where a new state would be created as their
national homeland. An even larger number left Europe for
other destinations. They were convinced that there was
no future in the Old World and left to find a place in the
New. Attacks called pogroms, often encouraged by the
czar's authorities, broke out in many parts of the Russian
Empire. Hundreds of thousands of Jews left, which pleased
the Russians; sometimes it seemed as if whole villages
were transplanted to America, South Africa, or Australia.

For his part, Henryk was firmly tied to Poland, and
working for change there. When he received his medical
degree in 1903, the political climate was explosive. Although he had just begun his first job as doctor at the
Berson and Bauman Children's Hospital—a clinic for Jewish children, endowed by two philanthropists—he was
taken into the Russian army to serve in a war that had
broken out against Japan. The Russian Empire spread
halfway across the world, and its eastern borders were in
conflict with Japan's. Each nation wanted to dominate
trade in the Pacific and grab parts of the weak Chinese
Empire.

In that war, which lasted until 1905, Henryk traveled
thousands of miles across two continents as an army
doctor. He received an education, in primitive medical
conditions, beyond anything he had known in Warsaw.
As a young physician who had only recently begun
practicing, he was put to the test immediately.

At first Henryk had conflicting feelings. He knew that
conditions in the army were terrible and that thousands
of Russian soldiers—many of them Poles, Jews, and other
minorities—were dying from lack of care in far-off Siberia.
It was his duty to help them. But as a Polish nationalist

he realized that if Russia fell, his own nation could rise again, free.

Then, too, it hadn't been easy to find the position at the hospital he now had to leave. For several months he had despaired that no one would hire him because of his reputation for being a radical. Hospitals were organizations where everyone had to work together smoothly, and those in positions of power were suspicious of him.

In his blackest moments, he had found himself considering suicide again. What good was all his training if he couldn't go to work? When he turned to his family, he found his mother still locked in her memories of the past and his sister Anna mourning the end of a disastrous love affair.

Feeling blocked, his future at a standstill just when he wanted to go the fastest, Henryk poured his frustrations into a sequel to his first book on the city slum children. This time he concentrated on upper-class life, the privileges he had known in his own distant youth, before Jozef's collapse. The book, *The Drawing Room Child*, was published in 1904 while he was still serving in the Russo-Japanese War. It makes clear the distance between pampered life in a drawing room, where a boy surrounded by falseness and snobbery longs to be free, and real life in the world of hunger and poverty where the masses face the same questions each day:

How can they keep the family together? Pay for the room, for food, clothes, washing, candles, doctor, druggist, and the priest for a burial—even occasionally get drunk and throw a party? Now I understand why those children have gray skins like prisoners, bowed legs, and why of ten born under these roofs only four will survive. What I do not understand is how those four ever grow up and have the strength to work at all.

The book was published in installments, and like his other essays and satires, under the name Korczak. Many fashionable people read it, even though it criticized them. But his new fame was no help in locating a job; he had to be careful to stay on the right side of the Russian authorities, who banned all political activity in Poland. They were always ready to throw a young radical into a prison or dank fortress. They watched the Jews especially carefully, and clashes with the police were frequent. Henryk knew some of his classmates who were imprisoned for years at a time. If this happened to him, who would take up his duties among the poor?

After he began work at the hospital, he had to drop everything to fight. He was sent thousands of miles, over the Ural Mountains, into Asia. The Trans-Siberian Railroad had just been completed, the world's longest train line, after more than fifteen years of work; some said the war was being fought only to protect the immense investment the czar had made in extending his empire to the Pacific. Such a distance to travel for a futile cause!

Then, to the humiliation of the Russians, the war was soon over. Their forces were easily beaten by the Japanese. In a large naval battle, the whole Russian fleet was destroyed, and on land, they did no better. United States president Theodore Roosevelt helped negotiate the peace terms by which Russia had to accept complete defeat.

This loss of face encouraged those who wished to bring down the government. Radical protests took place in European Russia, and Henryk's forces were hurried back to cope with the unrest. Was this the revolution come at last?

It appeared so when, in January 1905, a crowd of peaceful demonstrators was massacred in the imperial city of Saint Petersburg. The entire country seemed aflame, and in the unhappy areas like Poland, where the Russians ruled as conquerors, the rebels were especially daring.

By the time peace was partially restored, Czar Nicholas II had agreed to a few moderate reforms in order to preserve his kingdom. Steps were taken toward writing a constitution and forming a government to represent some of the people. But most of the radicals were kept in prison, and their followers had to pledge secretly to carry on the fight. Hopes for an independent Poland had to be deferred a while longer.

Henryk returned to Warsaw and his position, wearing the Russian army uniform for a time. As the only doctor in residence, he lived in an attic room and received a small salary. He depended upon his mother to manage his resources and make the money last.

When he had to, he accepted calls from wealthy families in order to treat pampered children who often reminded him of himself as a boy or of the children he had criticized in his book. But he knew that the children were in no way responsible: Their mothers were only curious and willing to pay to meet the angry young doctor whom everyone was talking about.

He wasted as little time as necessary in these homes. A wealthy manufacturer, a general high in the army, Jews and Christians alike—it was all the same to him. He was rude to the parents: When one woman asked him what he was writing these days, hoping to be able to tell her friends in advance about his newest novel, he merely snapped at her, "Prescriptions, Madam."

He found these people lacked common sense, in spite of all their wealth. They would ask how long a child should sleep, how much he should eat. Henryk would merely reply in his most matter-of-fact voice, "Until he wakes up—until he's full." He would also have liked to tell them that a child would never be hurt by a bit of dust or disorder, but could have his imagination and joy in life smothered by all their restrictions. He spent as much time as he could with the unhappy children themselves, who lay in overheated luxury, being made to swallow tonics to build them up, when all they wanted was to be outside playing. No wonder their systems were weak.

The sharper he was with their parents, and the more he asked in fees, the more they called for him. So he took their money, a beginner charging as much as noted specialists—and to his amazement, getting it without a complaint. He felt better when he realized that this enabled him to treat the poverty-stricken for almost nothing. He remembered the old saying "To a sick man, a free doctor is worthless," so he was always careful to charge everyone something, even the poorest. Paid-for care preserved dignity and possibly even helped them to recover. How often, too, they would find left behind, as if by accident, a small sum to pay for the medicine he prescribed.

One way or another, he made sure he was doing all he could in the struggle that went on eternally between weak and strong, rich and poor. He even risked his career by secretly nursing Poles wounded in the uprisings against the Russians—while he was still in the Russian army. If this had been known, he might have been put in jail.

He also refused to stay in the officers' quarters on the train back from the war. The officers had been given comfortable compartments, but the common soldiers were crammed into packed and evil-smelling berths. Many were dying or wounded, without food or water for days. When Henryk saw these conditions, he took his own gear and forced his way into the miserable cabins. He stayed up for nights sharing his provisions and reading to the frightened men from a book of Russian poetry he had brought with him. He changed bandages and dressings, and performed excruciating amputations when he had to.

In his mind he kept seeing the waste and futility of war. As the train passed through destroyed Manchurian and Chinese villages, he saw abandoned children everywhere. The troops stopped for a time, and Henryk went to see a school. He was horrified at the long cane used for discipline, and cringed when he had to ride in a man-drawn rickshaw.

He could recall the few words of Chinese that Iuo-Ya, a four-year-old, had taught him. How he had wanted to stay in her village and help her family rebuild their shattered hut.

The brutality of war came down hardest on people like these who could do nothing about it. As a result of what he experienced, Henryk remained a pacifist all his life. Each time he was made to serve, he came to detest violence all the more. War went against everything he hoped to achieve; it further crippled the weak and helped the strong. As he told the men on the train, "Always think first of the child before you make a revolution!" The principles that were to lead him in the future were already formed in these chaotic days.

9

Stefa

Deeply marked by his wartime experiences, Henryk worked for several more years at the Berson and Bauman Children's Hospital in Warsaw. He was glad to have a regular position but was always thinking of ways to broaden his impact on society even more. Dispensing medicine to the sick was but one part of what he hoped to achieve.

He found great satisfaction in being the first to take poor children to camps at the shore or in the mountains. Philanthropists had given money to establish two summer camps for slum children—one for Jewish and one for Christian, as required—and Henryk was there as the doctor in residence. Although he would have preferred to combine the facilities, he understood that until Polish society changed a great deal more, such segregation would remain.

All his life, even after he became famous as Janusz Korczak, he retained the simple love for the outdoors, developed during these summers. He remembered the

Korczak with children and other staff at a summer
camp POLISH KORCZAK ASSOCIATION

A group of campers working outside POLISH KORCZAK
ASSOCIATION

serenity of nature and the escape from the unhealthy
conditions of city life. The Polish countryside was un-
spoiled, food from the land was plentiful, and the children
blossomed like the fields themselves. All the energies that
had been cramped into small rooms and alleys were
released, and it even became easier to teach them.

They sang while they gathered fruits and berries, they
learned from nature just from being in it, and they
developed more in that short time than during the whole
year in Warsaw. Henryk would have made the summers
last forever if he could have.

As his own thirst for knowledge kept growing, he
decided to leave Poland again, but this time of his own
free will. To be a better doctor, he would have to go
abroad for further study not available in Warsaw. He had
saved just enough from his earnings to finance a few

months each in Paris, Berlin, and London. Once in these
cities, he slept little, for every moment was precious.
Hours were spent at the medical schools, and in libraries
that offered materials he badly needed.

He learned the latest pediatric theories and new medical
techniques, and spoke with doctors and students about
how he could use what he had observed. He was eager
to return to Warsaw, even though he knew that he might
never be able to see these places again. To accomplish
more than the average student might, in each city he also
found ways to visit orphanages, clinics, and schools.
Inhabitants seldom went there, much less a foreigner from
provincial Warsaw. But Henryk was determined to see
how more advanced countries treated their needy.

In his memoirs, years later, he remembered these as
days of want and dreams: "Often two glasses of milk and
a slice of bread were my whole diet. . . . I kept hoping I
wasn't polishing the clinic floors of European capitals with
my tired feet only to discover I did it just to fill up my
life's cup with disappointment."

During this period, Henryk knew he faced a critical
choice, one he would have to act upon when he returned.
He would be a more skilled doctor than before, and
probably even more in demand. His practice as a pediatrician could grow as much as he was willing to work at it.
His other career as a writer of social criticism could also
be cultivated, because the wealthy liked having a doctor
who was famous and clever. He could become independent and comfortable.

But he knew that this was not enough, for unless he
could get closer to those in need who would never dream
of coming to a prominent doctor, he would never be
satisfied. Yes, he had managed to balance his different
selves, to write and to heal the sick; he had also succeeded
in supporting his family and putting the tragedy of his
father's collapse largely behind them. But he still had the

Korczak as a young doctor and author
POLAND MAGAZINE

old longing to change society for the better and make something important out of what others viewed as wasted lives.

As he reached thirty, he felt he had put too many bandages on the infections of society rather than removing the causes of the wounds themselves. He was impatient to find a way to enter the battle for social justice on the side of the weak, and bring dignity and health to the needy.

Henryk's perceptions of the future he might build in Poland were also sharpened by a meeting he had in Switzerland with an unusual woman a few years younger than himself. Stefania Wilczynska came from a Polish-

Jewish background similar to his but without his child-hood trauma. Her family was extremely assimilated and very well off. She had chosen to go abroad alone for her education, an unusual step for a young woman then.

But Stefa had many out-of-the-ordinary abilities. She knew several languages, had attended university in Belgium, and excelled in her studies everywhere. She was completely modern in her attitudes and believed that her obvious physical plainness was unimportant. She was determined to have a dynamic and useful career entirely on her own and, like Henryk, was highly patriotic about the future of Poland.

Her Jewishness also mattered little to her. Her family exerted no pressures on her to conform; they knew she had decided to be completely independent and would go her own way. She was tall and dark, with a strong face that came alive with pleasure when her mind was touched. She loved to discuss her ideas and hopes for the future and had a deep appreciation of poetry and the life of the imagination. Like Henryk, she nourished a great dream of working for social betterment.

Hoping that she would understand him, Henryk spoke to her openly on the park bench beside the lake where they met. He told her of his doubts that he could find the strength to achieve his aims and still live a traditional existence: "What right have I, a Polish Jew living under Russian rule and not much better than a slave, to have children and a family of my own? It's better that I make no attachments to anything and put all my energy into doing something about things that can be changed. As my child, I'll choose the idea of serving all children."

Stefa felt an unusually deep emotion upon hearing these words from the intense young doctor she had known so briefly. He seemed to have a lively zest for life and told her all about his travels. She realized that he was much less committed to politics than she was, but she hadn't

Stefania Wilczynska KIBBUTZ
LOHAMEI HAGHETAOT

imagined that his devotion to medicine blocked out every-thing else, including a personal relationship.

When she learned that he was also Korczak, the author of the clever satires she had read in Warsaw, she was amazed that he had done so much already, yet seemed so frustrated. Their conversation made her realize that she too was impatient with the abstract political discussions she had heard among the exiled students in Switzerland; she too wanted to act, now.

Henryk spoke to her again: "Something draws me back to Warsaw. I love the Vistula; I think it's more beautiful than the Seine or the Danube even though people sing such romantic songs about them. I've seen real beauty in the Polish countryside, too, but it's city life I have to get

back to. I want to learn as much as I can outside of
Poland, but only to use it there. I can't let myself even
feel as if I'm running away. There's so much I want to
do."

Now Stefa felt she understood the upheavals of Henryk's youth. He had held nothing back from her—the
terrible memories of his father's exile to mental asylums
and his death in the last one. When she told him she was
certain that no modern mind like his could really believe,
as he claimed, that he was doomed to carry this seed of
insanity with him forever, Henryk replied, "I know it's
not scientific, but I feel I have a special fate I can't escape.
I know that I'm not like most other people. I stopped
wanting to be a long time ago."

Stefa exclaimed, with a toss of her dark head, "Well,
do you think I am? I should surely say not; I never
wanted to be. If I did, I'd be back in Warsaw now waiting
for my mother to find me some eligible young man from
our circle. No thank you." Her dark eyes flashed proudly,
then glanced down.

"Stefa—may I call you that?—I think *you* can understand what I mean. You can see that I have no choice but
to be different. I'm the son of a madman. Sometimes I
want things for myself, but then I realize I'm better off
with nothing, because I can't lose anything. It's life I want
to change; I want to make things completely upside-down
in Poland. We can't let things stay the way they are."

Stefa answered, "But you know, there are a lot of
people who talk the way you do. Everybody here our age
talks about communism; it's going to put the bottom on
top, just as you want."

"No, Stefa, I don't want to substitute one political
system for another. All that does is make the weak even
weaker. I want to make them safe and strong, for good. I
think maybe my father saw this too, but he was afraid if
he tried to do it, the people in their social class would

reject him. And he had responsibilities to my mother and me, and my sister. That's why I want nothing for myself; it's better that way. You know what Karl Marx wanted for the workers of the world?—I want that for the children!"

When he saw Stefa's smile, Henryk told her he knew it sounded crazy. But he was certain that only the children he knew from the slums of Warsaw could be trusted to lead the revolution he had in mind. "I wouldn't trust anybody else to run my new Republic!"

After a moment, Stefa broke the silence that had grown between them. "It's not so different, you know, from what the other students here say. You want to lead a revolution too—of the children! I can see what you mean, but why does that have to rule out a life of your own?"

Henryk thought for a time: "I know there are beautiful things to be enjoyed in life, and believe me, I've done some of them. But I know that I have just so much time and energy. I belong to all the children, not just a few that I might one day call my own. I want to change things for all of them, because if I can't, then things will never be any better, not in Poland, and not anywhere else."

He went on: "Nobody really thinks about the rights of children until something goes wrong, but I know this: You cannot have healthy adults if there are sick children. All you'll have is a crippled world. And education isn't just for kids—it's all life long. We've *got* to break through the generations to stop things from just going on and on. . . ."

Stefa had heard radical ideas discussed in coffeehouses and student cafés all over Europe, but no one had ever said such things about children. She was fascinated with this strange young doctor. Although he spoke of doing away with the individual, he was full of personal magnetism. And, though he was insignificant in appearance, his words had the force of steel.

Stefa saw in him the man she had always hoped to

meet, who wouldn't be concerned about her lack of
ordinary beauty and who would lead the way for her to
accomplish something unique with her own life. She knew
that she would never be satisfied with a traditional woman's role, and for that reason she hoped to find other
unusual people. She was not certain where her independence would lead her, but in Henryk she saw a guide.
What had she been preparing herself for if not such a
brave adventure as he seemed to be planning?

Stefa knew that Henryk would return to Warsaw soon.
She would not be staying in Switzerland much longer
herself. When he resumed his position at the hospital,
perhaps she would see him there, for she was related to
several prominent doctors. She knew that with such a
start to his career, he could accomplish wonderful things.
His idea for a Children's Republic appealed to her greatly.
She agreed with his description of children as the power-
less victims of adult mistakes, and although she understood that some of his passion came from his own unhappy
past, she was ready to help in his fight and make it a
bond between them.

Although she and Henryk also shared a common Jewish
heritage, each had dispensed with formal religion and
assumed that their future would involve no continued
Jewish identity. Yet for both of them, the desire to
improve conditions for all minorities had begun with an
awareness of their own shaky position as Jews within
Polish society. All their efforts were directed toward the
ideal of breaking the traditional patterns of separation and
rejection of the Jews as a despised race, always in danger.

As Henryk said, the Jews had been like orphans in
Poland too long, just as Poland itself had been victimized
by other nations. These conditions were so ancient that,
to believe, as they both did, that one or two people could
change them also formed a great bond of optimism between them.

Henryk had admitted, "I know that I must be abnormal, to feel the way I do. My father was abnormal, and look how he wound up. But I won't be beaten, like he was; I want to rise *above* normalcy! I want to give the power of change to children. Adults have made a mess of things for too long."

Years later he wrote, "I've been in four wars. I've seen men with limbs blown off and stomachs ripped open. But I tell you, I've never seen a crueler sight than a drunk beating a child or a kid begging in a tavern, 'Papa, come home.' This is the war that never stops: the adult world's wickedness against the child."

Of everything that Henryk said to her, one thing touched Stefa the most: "Children can be orphans, you know, even when their parents are living. If they never achieve what they might have been in their lives, then they are orphaned from themselves, and that is the worst loss of all."

While she knew that he was really talking about his own unhappy childhood, even before Jozef's sickness, now Stefa realized that loneliness and isolation had always been the enemies for them both. True, her own youth had been more normal on the surface, but when she thought about it, she realized that she too had been made by society to deny herself what she really wanted and what she could do best. It had been done more gently, yes, but the result was still to push down her ideals and her individuality. Now she was resolved to change, to matter.

Henryk's future would be hers too. She was eager to know what he would do after he returned to Warsaw. She knew that he would find a true test for his beliefs.

10

The Orphans' Home at Last

Henryk did not have to wait long before the last piece appeared in the pattern that formed the various parts of his life. While he had been abroad, the Jews of Warsaw had discovered that a new facility was needed to care for the homeless children of the community. On Dzika Street, the only orphanage they currently supported was close to useless. Reports reached them that conditions were becoming intolerable. The growing Jewish population of Warsaw was being increasingly squeezed between the Poles and the Russians as political tensions mounted, and the homeless children were in desperate need of help. Rumors circulated that the money raised to help them was being misused, even stolen.

One day, a delegation paid an unannounced visit to the orphanage; they were horrified at what they saw. Naked and emaciated children sat or lay listlessly in terrible filth. No toys, no bedding, only scraps of food. Meanwhile the well-fed staff ate roast goose in the comfortable kitchen and warmed themselves with expensive liqueurs.

A hurried meeting of Jewish community leaders was called to deal with the abuses, and a decision was reached to take emergency measures. The children were moved out to a temporary refuge in a former convent at the northern edge of the city. The corrupt staff from Dzika Street were all fired, and conditions in the new home on Franciszkanska Street were watched carefully.

People began talking about the need to build a new permanent shelter. A leader of the community, the well-known doctor Isaac Eliasberg, asked his niece Stefa Wilczynska, then twenty-five and recently returned from Switzerland, to help run the temporary home, and she gave her energies willingly. She and Henryk had met again at a party given to help raise funds for the new building and alert the whole community to what needed to be done.

Henryk and Stefa were delighted to see each other again. She told him what had happened on Dzika Street, and he was outraged. The children now looked so much better, and he felt his heart open to them. Although he was glad to be back at the hospital, he didn't want to be only with the sick. As he put it, "A spoonful of tonic can never cure poverty or being parentless." He himself was just past thirty, and he sought out Dr. Eliasberg to tell him he wanted to help as much as he could.

He told the older man that he was prepared to give up his position as well as the future of a rich practice on the outside. He wanted more than anything else to be in on the design of an ideal children's home. As a pediatrician, he could provide the medical care needed for the children, but the opportunity to build, from the ground up, a totally new world for the orphans was more important still.

He asked Dr. Eliasberg to give him a free hand in

Korczak, *left*, with Dr. Eliasberg and Stefa KIBBUTZ LO-
HAMEI HAGHETAOT

planning key elements in the design and administration of the home. In exchange, he was willing to give his entire life to it.

Over the next three years, until the Orphans' Home was officially opened in 1913, Henryk went on working at the hospital, counting the days until the orphans and abandoned boys and girls would move into the building that was soon to become a landmark in Warsaw. A large lot had been purchased at 92 Krochmalna Street, a busy thoroughfare in a working-class district of mixed Jewish and Christian population, where "the very paving stones groaned from poverty."

By coincidence, at the same time the building was being constructed, the family of Isaac Bashevis Singer, who seventy years later won the Nobel Prize in literature for his Yiddish stories and novels, moved to Krochmalna Street from a small rural town in Poland. The Singers lived further down Krochmalna, several blocks away, until

The original Orphans' Home   KIBBUTZ LOHAMEI HAGHETAOT

the outbreak of World War I. Singer, though then a small child, remembers the high esteem in which the orphanage was held by the poor Jews of Warsaw. When the building was completed, and Korczak, as Henryk was becoming increasingly known, took over as director, there was nothing comparable in all Poland.

Korczak was then thirty-three. He resigned his other duties and committed himself fully to providing the one hundred children who were the home's first occupants with the best possible conditions. Not all were actually orphans in the sense of having no parents; many had been abandoned or had deserted homes where they were unwanted and neglected to the point of illness.

Years later, Korczak recalled his mixed feelings about ending his career in medicine then. Had he betrayed his duty as a doctor in leaving the hospital for the orphanage? What about his promise to his father and himself to provide comforts for his family? He had left security for the constant challenge of managing difficult problem children—outcasts and rejects of society. There were surely dangers ahead.

But he knew that he had never really been satisfied as a doctor. He often clashed with the traditional physicians, who resented him. He was insulting and offensive when he came across unscrupulous or incompetent doctors who victimized the helpless. He told people what he felt, no matter their hurt feelings, especially when the rights of children were at stake. He even sometimes broke the law by refusing to sign his prescriptions with the title Doctor.

He felt pulled in two directions: "I deserted medicine, I deserted the bedsides of sick children, I abandoned the medical profession to become—of all things—a sculptor of the child's soul, to find myself afloat in unknown waters! In so doing, I arrived at the world's greatest hurdle: guiding the future for the healthy child."

The orphanage on Krochmalna Street as it looks today, somewhat plainer than before the war, and with a monument to Korczak in front POLISH KORCZAK ASSOCIATION

Once the home on Krochmalna Street was filled with boys and girls from seven to fourteen, Korczak's schedule was too busy to permit such self-doubts. The building was a source of immense pride. It was so solidly constructed that it was one of the very few that would survive the terrible bombings of Warsaw in World War II. Although all its inhabitants would be killed, it would remain sound.

Korczak and Stefa gave the architects definite ideas for what they wanted included. The orphanage was built with a line of thirty-six five-foot-high windows facing the busy street, to provide natural light at all times, but it was set back in a spacious cobblestone yard for quiet. The children could be seen playing on the grounds with rabbits and other small pets.

Inside, in the bright and airy central hall, the children ate together. There was a piano in the hall, and all functions were held there. A balcony overlooked the room; there was heating, and modern bathroom and kitchen

A view of the central hall on the first floor of the home, where all common activities took place   KIBBUTZ LOHAMEI HAGHETAOT

facilities for the children, many of whom had been living on the street. The entire building radiated warmth and light, without luxury or waste. The children felt secure under the watchful eyes of Pan Doktor and Miss Stefa.

They slept on high-backed metal cots in large open rooms, which Korczak later judged as giving too little privacy. As he became more aware of their needs by actually living with them year after year, he decided that it might have been better to provide the children with small private rooms, rather than the communal quarters he first had thought would bring them closer together.

He himself occupied a partitioned-off room—his "cage"—between the boys' and girls' dormitories, with windows opening into both so that he was accessible to them all in the night when a sick or wakeful child might disturb the others. Medical supplies were kept there and minor ailments treated. It was furnished with just a few possessions, mostly books and writing materials—and his father's

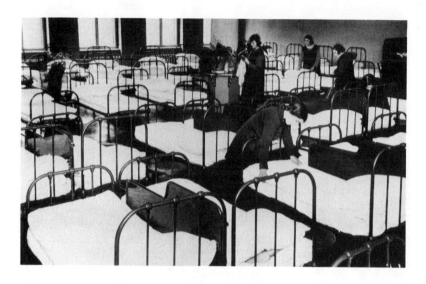

Inside the girls' dormitory at the home   KIBBUTZ LOHAMEI HAGHETAOT

desk, kept from the old apartment so many years before.

Korczak went about in clothes so worn that he was often taken for the janitor by the many visitors who came to see the famous building. More than once he had coins pressed into his hand after he appeared, carrying a dish towel, to help a richly dressed woman off with her coat or take a gentleman's hat. And he always wore an old green apron over his clothes so that he could do whatever real work needed doing. As he explained, "These days the color of excitement and revolution seems to be red, but I prefer green. To me, it's youth and hope; the color of the future I want for the children."

11

Our Home

In the first years of its operation, before Korczak was called again to war, this time in 1914, the Orphans' Home grew rapidly. The older children left at age fourteen, but remained as part of the greater family structure. Korczak arranged apprenticeships for them, or jobs on farms to prepare them to live in the world outside the home. He was sensitive to criticisms of coddling them, and also had to be certain that there would be room for the new children who showed up regularly. Only a few were allowed to stay past age fourteen, in exchange for tutoring or supervising the others. Some of these later became teachers and stayed for years.

He and Stefa worked together closely—often eighteen hours every day—at the countless tasks of daily operation, with little help from any adults except a cook, house-keeper, and the real janitor. Every child had a definite job on the grounds or inside—kitchen, bathrooms, dormitory cleanup—and all duties were shared and rotated. Visitors

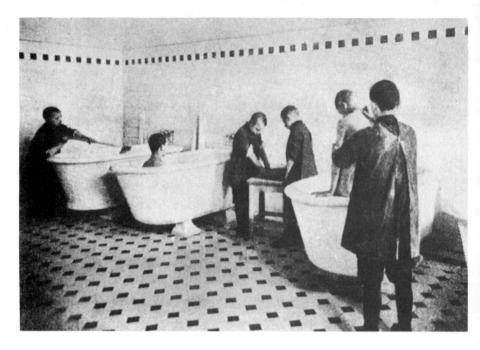

Children helped each other to keep clean at the home.
KIBBUTZ LOHAMEI HAGHETAOT

were amazed at the efficiency and cleanliness, each person shouldering his or her responsibilities with a minimum of trouble and expense.

The doctor himself, as director, tended to all the physical needs of the children. He kept scrupulous records of weights, and for measuring heights used a gold ruler given to him for his services in the Japanese War. Such valuables were rare, but to him were merely useful tools. He treated all injuries and sicknesses, clipped nails, washed and scrubbed those too young to take care of themselves. He cut the children's hair, sometimes doing it in funny patterns resembling the streets of the city, to calm boys who had never sat for a haircut before.

He was especially concerned that the children keep their shoes clean and comfortable. He loved to cobble, repairing

The children took good care of their possessions at the home. KIBBUTZ LOHAMEI HAGHETAOT

the shoes in a little basement workshop, and he taught the children how to do it themselves. But when the shoes were fixed again, woe to whoever didn't keep his neat!

To Korczak, honest labor and pride in simple possessions were so important that they formed a kind of religion. At the home, the cook, the laundress, and the janitor came to meetings. Their opinions were valued and listened to; after all, they had as much daily contact with the children as anyone. "To me, they're equals," Korczak said. "All honest workers have clean hands."

The children were expected to work and master simple tasks, rather than rely on others to do things for them. At meals, they cleared their own places and kept their bowls and utensils in order. Their shoes, dishes, and spoons were checked carefully to see how they cared for things.

Some thought this was eccentric, but Korczak knew you could sometimes learn the most from the smallest things— how people ate, their posture, how they walked.

Remembering the terrible scenes of his own childhood, he was also proud that his children protected one another in times of need. One boy suffered from epilepsy and sometimes had seizures on his way to school through a tough Christian neighborhood. The older boys would form a circle around him if he fell in a fit, and when the bullies attacked, they took the blows together until he was ready to go on. No one ever need really be alone.

After only a few years of operation, a difficult period arrived for the home when World War I broke out. As Dr. Goldszmit, Korczak was again called to service in the Russian army, and Warsaw itself was invaded by the German soldiers advancing eastward. During his absence the children were left entirely to the care of Stefa, and what they had hoped would be a short time turned into many months.

Stefa was fully capable of the challenge. During the troublesome time of the German occupation from 1915 to 1918, despite occasional food shortages, she kept things going just as she and Korczak had planned. The German High Command even visited, having heard of the famous pair and their independent family of orphans. They left highly impressed by this extraordinary young woman who ran the home firmly but lovingly. When they wanted to speak to her personally, she told them she hadn't the time: "I have no personal matters. Everything concerns the children." To the youngsters she seemed more organized and disciplined than the doctor. He was a man of ideals; she at least remembered names.

Korczak, in the meantime, was stationed in Kiev, a large city, capital of the Russian province of the Ukraine. Tensions were very high there because the nationalistic

Ukrainians wanted independence as much as the Poles, and the Germans threatened to overrun the area. Kiev also had a very large Jewish population, and the Jews were afraid of being caught among all the warring factions, none of which they trusted. Conditions were terrible, and as usual, thousands of children had been orphaned or abandoned. Korczak was horrified and wrote in his diary of the war:

> Kiev—all is chaos. Yesterday the Communists. Today the Ukrainians. The Germans come nearer and nearer, and the whole of Russia is in turmoil.
>
> Murders were an everyday affair. . . . How naive my own efforts seem: From a sense of duty I tried my best to save the children. They were covered with ulcers and scabs. Their eyes were sore from malnutrition and malnourishment. There was no one to look after them, so the authorities allocated an instructress of embroidery! What graft and robbery! Human language hasn't invented terms strong enough to denounce the situation.

In the months he stayed in Kiev, he met many Poles living in exile. One, Mrs. Maryna Falska, was an active Socialist who ran an orphanage for Polish children. Korczak spent as much time as he could there, helping with the children and trying to protect them from the war going on all around them. He and Maryna Falska became lifelong comrades because of their work together during the war in Kiev. After the war, when she returned to Poland, she founded, with his help, an orphanage for working-class children in Pruszkow, then in the Warsaw suburb of Bielany.

In the reborn and independent Polish state, created in 1919, Jewish and Christian institutions still had to be separate. Although this new orphanage was only for non-

Jews, Korczak played an active role in running Our Home, as he called it. For fifteen years he divided his time between the two places, and put his ideas into practice in both equally. When, in 1936, the growing menace of anti-Semitism within Poland forced him to be removed from his duties at Our Home, this was a troubling indication of the hatred that was soon to engulf Poland and all of Europe.

12

How to Love a Child

It was in Kiev that Korczak wrote *How to Love a Child*, which was his most complete statement of principles on the ideal methods of raising children for a better future. He already had several years' experience running the Orphans' Home in Warsaw, but seeing the overwhelming brutality of World War I firsthand proved to him that the powers of destruction were sometimes stronger than the greatest dreams and had to be fought in real terms. He felt the need to write a work that would give useful information on how better conditions could be achieved in Poland once it was a free nation again. *How to Love a Child* is the best expression of Korczak's famous idea of establishing a Children's Republic as an alternative to the way the world had always treated the defenseless.

Basically, his beliefs center on the principle that the child is entitled to the same respect that adults expect for themselves but rarely if ever give to others. Children were capable of great accomplishments, he was sure, but they had to be permitted to manage their own affairs with as much independence as possible. He was convinced that they, being uncorrupted, would show more responsibility than adults.

Korczak knew that discipline, as much as he disliked it, would still be needed. But he preferred that the children themselves employ it. He believed that from biblical and ancient times to the present, adults had always overlooked children or taken advantage of them for profit. But never had they recognized the special state of the child—not a miniature adult or a helpless creature—but an independent person of a particular age and wholeness.

He wrote, "Every moment of the child's life exists *now*, already, *not* in the future! He *is*; not 'will be.' Every event makes a lasting impression; every moment counts—none can ever be repeated." Korczak was convinced that children were the "true princes of feeling, the true poets and thinkers of the world."

In Kiev, to keep his own sanity, he labored at the book in every free moment, on and off the battlefield. *How to Love a Child* contains ideas that may be taken for granted now but that were far in advance of their time. It encourages self-esteem and love, rejects fear and punishment. It speaks of the need for a world constitution to protect the rights of children and an international declaration to make the nations observe it.

Although in Poland and elsewhere governments showed no actual interest in adopting such measures on their own, the League of Nations, which was formed after World War I to prevent another world war from happening, proclaimed a Declaration of the Rights of the Child in 1924. Then, in 1959, it was officially incorporated by the United Nations.

Today many people assume that the rights of minorities must be protected as part of civilized behavior, and in most countries laws make it illegal to discriminate racially or religiously, but Korczak was among the first individuals to stand up for the rights of any oppressed group. And he had more success in putting this belief into action in his orphanages than the League of Nations did in the outside world. When the United Nations established UN-ICEF in its permanent structure, it was in fact following in part what Korczak had proposed thirty years before: To make this the "Century of the Child: one-third of all work and all rewards should go to children, one-third of all humanity."

How to Love a Child is also important because it gives detailed descriptions of the two innovations, the Children's Court and Children's Parliament, which made the orphanages famous as the "most democratic republics in Europe." The book explains that qualified members could be elected to the parliament if no major charges of dishonesty were brought against them by the court, and if five others voted for them. The parliament was very important for Korczak's entire system because it gave the children a say in passing laws concerning the day-to-day operation of the home, including—and this was of special interest to the children—all work duties and time off.

Naturally, holidays were precious. The children worked hard almost every day because they were taught they had to be independent. They followed a demanding program, combining schoolwork—at the home for the younger ones and outside for the upper grades—with physical labor. Because of Korczak's and Stefa's attitudes, no religious holidays were celebrated, so a real day off was something very special. The parliament considered some of the following breaks, for example, which the children had suggested:

December 22, Not Worth Getting Up Day. Since the daylight was so brief, children could stay in bed as long as they wished.

June 22, Not Worth Going to Bed Day. Because of the brief night, they could stay up for twenty-four hours.

First Day of Snow Day. Reserved for tobogganing or snowballing.

Cook's 365th Dinner Preparation Day. A special dinner followed by sweets served for, not by, Cook.

Dirty Children's Day. No washing allowed.

Encouragement Day for Self-Improvement. Whoever has been found guilty of the most offenses during the year will be given a week's pardon, in which time he may act as the judge for the court!

We do not know if any of these holidays were adopted, but they received consideration, as did all the children's ideas.

Most importantly, at the very center of the self-rule system was the Children's Court of Peers. Because of Korczak's concern with promoting justice, which he had believed in strongly since childhood as the only way to settle disputes between the weak and the strong, he knew that some means would be needed to settle arguments that were bound to arise. He wanted the children to be able to settle their fights by themselves without his having to step in and use adult authority.

Although, of course, he encouraged peaceful ways, he was willing to let them battle each other physically if they felt they had to. But first they were obliged to register their complaint on paper and promise to fight fairly, no tricks or dirty blows. This simple plan helped to eliminate grudges or feuds from ever getting started, because most times the children didn't want to take the trouble to sign up for a fight and so found some other way of settling the matter.

The children in the home came from all types of back-

grounds, and Korczak knew that some would be cooperative and others would make problems. The self-governing
society of the children would have to be willing to use
discipline, just as he was, when it was absolutely needed.
In this way, when the children graduated from the home,
they would be more likely in their adult lives to treat
others fairly.

To encourage this, justice and order had to exist in the
home in a better form than in the outside world. The
court, composed of five members and a secretary, was at
the heart of this system because it protected everyone.
Over the years, thousands and thousands of cases were
brought. At one time or another, almost everyone was
charged. Korczak once counted to find the smallest number of cases in one week—50. The most—130.

As he described its beginnings, "Fatal for the court at
first were all the charges from small children over every
petty nonsense. Half were trivial disputes among the
youngest: 'Go on, sue me' became the usually heard
response to any little problem such as one child calling
another names, one wetting another by accident in the
toilet, one putting on another's jacket."

In time, the children learned not to bring such matters
to the court, and instead learned to use the standard of
"suffering inflicted"—just how deeply wronged did they
feel, and whether, after thinking about it for a time, did
they still feel determined to sue?

Occasionally, Korczak had to admit that certain children
were using the court to escape from their duties in the
home—"My case is up before the court day after tomorrow, so why should I bother to peel these potatoes?" or
"Why should I sweep the floor until I know how my case
comes out?"—and then he had to stop taking any further
complaints. Later, after a cooling-off period, he reinsti-
tuted the court on a trial basis.

It was also possible to sue the adults or bring charges

against oneself as a way of letting off steam. In six months, Korczak accused himself of losing his temper five times, slapping a child in frustration once, and suspecting another of petty theft once. In disciplining himself, he showed that he too had to learn control.

Once he even hurt someone by being too playful. The court records showed that the doctor was charged with placing a small boy on top of a tall wardrobe as a joke. When the boy complained, Korczak was judged guilty according to Code 100: "The offender admits to wrong and is given a minimum punishment if he will not repeat it." For some time after, Korczak was called Doktor 100.

In other cases, the rules—written by the children, in numbered paragraphs covering each type of wrong— called for publishing in the home newspaper the names of the more serious offenders. Code 800 removed all their privileges, and the final step, Code 1000, proclaimed, "Expulsion!" This happened only three times in twenty-five years.

But there was one last step before being expelled. If you were judged guilty of a Code 900 charge, you had three months' grace. You then had to find an older child with a good record, who would volunteer to be your sponsor. This meant that for three months he or she would be responsible for anything you did. Any punishments you got would go to that child instead, but afterward, he or she could recommend that you be put out. It was hard to find a sponsor, and if you did, hard to be good the whole time. Everyone dreaded being asked to serve or having to find somebody, so most of the children stayed clear of any big offenses. After all, they made the rules themselves, so there were no adults to blame.

How to Love a Child explains how this legal system hoped to build a better life for all:

The Court must defend the timid that they not be bothered by the strong. The Court must defend the hardworking and conscientious that they not be held back by the careless and idle.

The Court must see that there is order because disorder most harms the good and the quiet.

The Court must see that the big do not bully, and that the small do not make themselves a nuisance to the big. That the clever do not take advantage of the less clever. That the bad-tempered do not annoy and that they are not teased by the others. That the happy do not joke the sad.

The Court is not justice but tries for it. It is not truth but wants it.

How to Love a Child also describes Korczak's idea for a division of labor, which was so important at both homes. The children had to be responsible for their own things, since the few adults could not possibly take charge of everything. They kept their treasures—pictures of lost parents, tattered ribbons from broken-down dolls, seashells from trips to the shore—as their own property, safe in lockers, but when things sometimes disappeared, there was a lost-and-found, and a cooperative toy exchange for swapping what they no longer wanted. They ran their own store, established a newspaper and magazine, and performed all the jobs usually done by adults. Unlike their normal tasks in the kitchen or dormitories, for which they were unpaid, these special jobs brought them adult wages and privileges.

Money was watched carefully at the Orphans' Home. Leading Jewish philanthropists considered it impressive to be listed on the rolls of contributors who supplied the working capital. Korczak himself did not have the time or heart to engage in fund-raising, leaving this task mostly

The children at the store they ran in the home   KIBBUTZ
LOHAMEI HAGHETAOT

to Stefa. Once he even had to refuse donations from sources he considered not quite respectable, so perhaps it was better if he didn't know exactly where all the funds came from.

For especially responsible behavior and to encourage a sense of worth, the children got credits toward earning beautifully engraved jubilee postcards, colored scenes of flowers, animals, and landscapes. For rising early in winter, a snowscape. In spring, a flower scene. Many kept these cards as mementos all their lives. When they left the home, all their comrades would sign and present them with a special forget-me-not card, often a picture of Warsaw, to keep forever, wherever they might go.

Soon after its publication, *How to Love a Child* became a great success even though it had a curious style, like the random thoughts of a person talking to himself. Most of the ideas in it came from Korczak's accomplishments while helping Maryna Falska. When he had first arrived in Kiev, the children had been idle and miserable; discipline was a major problem. He instituted useful training in shoemaking, tailoring, bookbinding, and plumbing, to prepare them for the future. They were put in charge of their own order and discipline, and chose leaders to police a court and control offenders. A newspaper was started to encourage them to express themselves.

They could also keep diaries, which Korczak invited them to show him every evening. But if anything was too personal, all they need do was mark the page with an X, and he would not touch it. They knew they could trust him.

The entire time Korczak helped Mrs. Falska, not a single child ran away or was injured, although the war was raging all over Kiev. Most had hated school before, and so were largely illiterate, but he taught them basic skills.

In many ways, Kiev was a proving ground for what he had begun to do before the war and hoped to resume in Poland afterward.

While the war went on, the Communist revolution started in 1917, and the Russian Empire began its final disintegration. Events were now taking place with great speed in Poland. Already Polish nationalists were planning for the new republic after more than a century of Russian rule. Would they be able to make changes? How would Poland make use of its first real chance for democracy? Stefa wrote Korczak what was occurring, and how she and the children needed him. Surely he'd been gone too long.

13

A Special Teacher

The years after the end of World War I in 1918 were filled with great changes. The map of Europe seemed totally redrawn as new and reborn countries, like Poland, appeared. The treaties that created them guaranteed stable democratic governments and the rights of all minorities, but racial and political troubles went on for many years. As usual, the good intentions on paper were ignored in reality.

Korczak and Stefa, both patriotic, assimilated Jews, had great hopes for the future of the new Polish state and its Jewish minority of more than one in ten. But human rights did not seem to have changed much for anyone, anywhere. Very soon, Poland became involved in another war, this time trying to expand its borders to the east, where both the Russians and Ukrainians fought them bitterly. Korczak was now an officer of the newly created Polish army, but the killing and waste of life were the same.

Poland had been re-created with more than one-third of its population composed of minorities who were neither Polish nor Catholic. Encouraged by fanatics who resented the minorities, riots broke out in many cities, often specifically directed against the Jews. Superpatriots accused them of having favored the German occupiers during the world war, or helping the Russian Communists now, or being disloyal by emigrating to Palestine or America. Nothing would have pleased the accusers more than if Poland could be rid of its three million plus Jews. Boycotts were organized against Jewish merchants and products, and bad feelings were everywhere.

The Polish president was assassinated in 1922, in part because he had Jewish support. Death to the President of the Jews had become a popular slogan. The new government even exceeded the old Russian one in passing laws to exclude Jews from jobs: Now they couldn't teach or work in state factories, railroads, or in the civil service system that ran the country and controlled the best positions. In the large Jewish quarters of the big cities, the old disputes continued over assimilation, socialism, and Zionism—the movement that preached a return to Palestine for all Jews. Warsaw was about one-third Jewish, and economic conditions were generally very bad, especially since many poor Jews had come from small country towns to find work that didn't exist. The numbers of needy children kept growing.

Korczak had to divide his time between the Jewish and Christian orphanages. He was sad to see that the children in both places were absorbing the tensions and hatred from the past. The older generations continued to poison the future.

When the Christian Our Home was opened, an anti-Semitic controversy erupted about him. The Jewish home on Krochmalna Street had been built to include a small chapel, for although Korczak and Stefa did not pray, they wanted it for children who came from traditional religious backgrounds and were without parents to turn to for comfort in a time of need. A rabbi even came to hold services on holidays for those who wanted to attend. Korczak and Stefa spoke only Polish in the home—not Yiddish, the first language of most of the children, and certainly not Hebrew—but they made sure that Jewishness was not totally absent from the atmosphere. Korczak said, "You can raise a child without religion, but not without God."

Because Korczak did not want to interfere with the children's religious identities or right to pray, he urged that a similar small chapel be built in Our Home, too, but Maryna Falska, who was very anti-religious, refused. When the Christian home was opened without one, violent attacks were written against him, the Jew Goldszmit. To many Poles, his rejection of his own religion made him a danger, an ungodly man, no matter how much he claimed to want only the best for the Christian children.

This was a bitter lesson for Korczak. He remembered how high his hopes had been when he first returned to Warsaw in 1919, after four years. Stefa had miraculously produced the supplies necessary to clean and tidy everyone and everything in sight. The children had stood in new smocks to recite their greetings; many of them had never seen the doctor. They were anxious to judge him against all the stories they had heard from the oldtimers who had known him before the war. Their cries of "Pan Doktor—he's come back to us" rang through the courtyard when he walked humbly in.

Stefa could see his joy to be back mixed with new strains lined on the familiar face. She knew the war had taken a big toll on him. He was now in middle age and they had both waited a long time, through all the inter-

Korczak with some of the younger children (several of the girls probably had their heads shaved after arriving at the home with lice) POLISH KORCZAK ASSOCIATION

ruptions, for the chance to put their ideals for a better Poland into practice. But the new conflicts with Poland's neighbors and the climate of hatred and persecution that was still so widespread meant that they had to be patient even longer.

In 1920, one of the older children, Josef Steinhart, was preparing to face his own future in the new country. His story, as told in a letter, is typical of the children who lived at the Orphans' Home at any given time. In Josef's case, he had been there almost from the beginning, arriving small and needy when the home was new, one of six orphaned brothers and sisters. He was accepted, but for a long time he was totally withdrawn:

> When I arrived there, I felt my whole world had collapsed; I withdrew into a shell. When I walked, I stared at the floor and wouldn't speak. In those days men's shirt collars were detachable and stiff, made of rubber or plastic to keep clean. Dr. Goldszmit (as I always called him) had me wear a high collar to force me to keep my head up high. But that didn't work because some of the children poked fun at me and I felt even worse. So he removed the collar and began to talk to me, personally, to build my confidence and convince me that I could handle any situation. He showed he cared about me as an individual, and that made the difference.

The seven-year-old boy was then given the ultimate status symbol at the home, a locker usually reserved for the older children, the only ones with keys. Soon the other young boys looked up to him, and his progress in adjusting to life in the home was rapid: "Dr. Goldszmit will always have a special place in my heart because he was a father to me at a time when I desperately needed one. He healed my physical and psychological ailments and instilled in me a code of ethics that I have kept all my life."

Josef Steinhart recalled that during the long period of Korczak's absence during the war, Stefa had occasional troubles with the boys, who were convinced that she favored the girls. She gave his own prized locker to a new girl arrival; he was furious and resented her for the rest of his time there. Only decades later did he see that she probably had an important reason for her action.

When Korczak first returned, one problem he had to face was this coolness of the boys toward Stefa. Josef recalls one brave boy who acted as a spokesman for them:

> He took Dr. Goldszmit aside the first chance he had and asked for a moment of private conversation. When the doctor agreed, the boy told him with greatest seriousness, "We have seen it, sir, all she has to do is blow in your ear, and you listen!"

Korczak knew that he would have to reassure the boys that neither he nor Stefa was in charge, one over the other. Now that he had returned, and he hoped for good, a balance would have to be restored, and the feeling of cooperation rebuilt. Josef remembered a particularly happy occasion soon after:

> One summer day, we boys were awakened at sunrise. We dressed quietly and sneaked out of the building, careful not to wake the girls in the next room. Once outside the main gate, we had transportation and food waiting for us. We spent the entire day in the country, where we had not been for the longest time during the war, playing games and having the greatest fun. How happy we were at having put one over on the girls! It agreed with all our ideas of secret adventure. This escapade provided a topic of conversation for months afterward. All the grumbling about Miss Stefa stopped: The home was back to normal.

In fact, such feelings of jealousy were unusual and probably caused by the long absence of the doctor. Many records speak of the extraordinary closeness between the boys and girls. They got along much better than they ever had in the outside world. At an age when they would normally have avoided each other at all costs, they shared goals and responsibilities, and learned to respect and love each other like a huge family:

> I felt the same closeness for many of the girls as I did for my own biological sister. I maintained a warm correspondence with some of them for over seventy years! In the home there were almost never any of the usual problems between boys and girls or young men and women. In this way too the Doctor succeeded in making a better world for us.
>
> As he said when we were together another time in the country, "Boys are like trees and girls like flowers here. When they're together, that's real harmony."

Being quite short, Josef was allowed to stay at the home until he was past fifteen. He attended a Polish vocational training school, because he had talent in technical drawing. Only a very few children from the home were permitted into such special schools, and when he and several others were graduated in 1920 they each received a special diploma they resented very much. It bore the heading "Society for Providing Work for Poor Jews," which the boys found humiliating.

They decided to protest. With Korczak's encouragement, they refused to accept the certificates, causing the authorities much embarrassment. Finally special copies were drawn up without the offensive title. The boys had a rare victory over the hostile officials of the Polish government.

The day finally arrived when Josef went to say goodbye to the doctor, having decided to leave the country and seek a better life elsewhere. Josef knew that he could stay in Warsaw and probably find work, and also be able to visit the home and his classmates as often as he wished, but he had real ambition for the future. As an orphan, he felt he had to make important decisions on his own, and be prepared to follow them through:

> I chose a Saturday, when the home was quieter than normal. I can still remember that beautiful July day in 1920, as we sat outside talking and reminiscing for a long time. I had decided to leave for America the following Monday.
>
> Conversation went smoothly until I mentioned that I was glad to leave, because I was convinced that Jews had no future in Poland.
>
> He thoroughly disagreed with me. He said vehemently that one day Poland would have a democratic government, and Jews could have a real place in it.
>
> I told him I was sure it would take two generations more of democracy to erase the deep anti-Semitism, and I couldn't wait that long. He said in such a case perhaps it was no great loss to the country for me to leave.

Josef was, of course, a bit hurt by the doctor's remark, but he knew that they had spoken as true equals, not as teacher and pupil. Each respected the other's opinion. Patriotism counted for a great deal to Korczak. He could not imagine life outside of Poland for very long. But just that week Josef had been shot at by a passing mob of hooligans and thrown off a streetcar with anti-Semitic curses. While walking peacefully on the street, his older brother had been stabbed when he ran into a group of Polish-American volunteers who had arrived to join the Polish army. Josef told the doctor how much he did not want to be sent to fight for a country that was persecuting him and his family. In America he would have a chance to start afresh, away from the centuries-old hatred.

Korczak tried again to convince Josef that Poland would

Korczak surrounded by children at the home *POLAND*
MAGAZINE

change in the coming years and that with his education
he would be in an excellent position to play a leading
role. But he could see that Josef's mind was made up:
"Very well, I won't try to keep you. If Poland won't miss
you, *I* certainly will!"

Each man did in fact always remember the other. Over
sixty years later in America, Josef Steinhart could recall

the quiet hour at the home when all organized activity and conversation stopped, and each child had to concentrate on his lessons and occupy himself silently, respectful of the others.

He remembered, too, the iodine that stained his hands one day when the children raided the big walnut tree in the yard before it was ready to be harvested. They didn't know dye was in the shell and would give them away when the doctor inspected their hands before supper that evening!

He recalled the time when no one could figure out who had taken something very special from one of the smallest girls. She bawled and bawled, but no one would confess. So the doctor spoke with each child, holding them casually by the hand until he could tell, by a sudden faster pulse, who had to get something off his mind—and later, in private, did!

This was the secret of Korczak's special teacher's love: Always save face for the child. Replace punishment and fear with understanding, forgiveness, and love. This love was not something to talk about, it was to do. It was rare, but it was real. The child was not living in a miniature or future world, but in an actual one. The adult teacher was not meant to boss, but to guide. As he put it, "You can't teach others until you've taught yourself. You don't tell a child to mop the floor until you've done it yourself, several times, to show him how, in the very best way."

14

New Challenges

In the 1920s in the new Polish republic, life for all the children in both homes was difficult. When they reached fourteen, most became graduates and had to make decisions regarding their futures. Like Josef Steinhart, many left for America, France, or Palestine. The majority chose to stay in Poland and build better lives.

Some of the children had close relatives in Poland—and some returned to their own parents who had not been able to care for them—but they all had the bonds established by living in the home. This extended family was often their closest tie. Proportionately more Jews lived in Poland than anywhere else in the world, but because of the difficulties of life in the newly independent country, there was nowhere they were less welcome.

Korczak's own existence was a mixture of optimism and doubt. The winters were unusually harsh and epidemics were frequent. He fought continually to keep the children healthy. When he was asked to help in the Polish army hospital for contagious diseases, he gladly took on the extra work, but caught the dreaded typhus germ that was killing thousands. He broke regulations by returning to his mother's apartment rather than risk exposing the children. He maintained the apartment for her, and also one for Anna, while he himself lived in the small room at the home. His mother carefully nursed him back to health, but caught the disease herself. While Korczak lay in a coma, the elderly woman died and her body was removed by a back staircase.

When he discovered what had happened, his despair was overwhelming. Korczak felt so guilty that he was paralyzed with grief, and he consulted a rabbi for comfort, which for him was unusual. He even tried reciting prayers that he wrote, for "those like me, who never pray," but nothing helped. He blamed himself for having neglected her in recent years in favor of the children, the orphans he knew he had put above her because of their needs. But now his mother was gone forever, and he himself was the orphan. And all because he had been careless— he, a doctor! Long after, he suffered from persistent nightmares in which he pictured her feverish death.

To forget his sorrow, he increased his work at the homes, trying to prepare the children for the difficult lives he knew they faced in the hostile Polish society. Once, while he was showing the Orphans' Home to a visitor, he indicated one particularly unhappy little girl for whom he had not been able to do much. "I took her out of a terrible home," he said, "but she'll have to go back to it at fourteen, and I know what her future will be: She'll be a prostitute like most of the other girls on her street. Her surroundings will undo all I was able to accomplish."

Another time, he took the children swimming in the country. A wealthy manufacturer, Maximilian Cohn, had given the home some cottages in honor of his late daughter Rosa. Korczak would take groups of the children for a

Korczak playing with an informal orchestra at summer camp
POLISH KORCZAK ASSOCIATION

month to Little Rose, as the camp was called. He took along a new female teacher to help him, but she was nervous when a few of the children acted a bit wild.

"What are you so uneasy about?" he asked. "Enjoy yourself."

"But doctor, someone might go down in the deep water, and I couldn't help. Nobody else is around."

"Now really, would that be such a terrible fate for a Jewish orphan in Poland? I ask you. Sometimes I think things couldn't get much worse," was his half-serious reply.

But for the most part, Korczak tried to be more optimistic. He became even better known when he wrote *King Matt the First,* his most famous work. This fable of a temporarily perfect land ruled by a boy-king summarizes many of his dreams and aspirations; it has been translated into more than twenty languages and is loved by children all over the world, as a story, a play, and a film. It appeals to everyone in its picture of a Utopia—an invented land where ideals usually found only in the imagination come true, for a while.

Matthew is a small prince who inherits the crown of an unnamed country when his father dies unexpectedly. Because he is innocent, he has the rare opportunity to found a Children's Republic, where all rules and responsibilities are the children's, while adults go back to school.

He is helped at first by Philip, a poor boy he sees playing soldier with other shabby children in the park. As king, naturally he cannot play with them as he wishes, so he sends Philip a note such as Korczak himself had wanted to write to the janitor's son many years before:

> Deere Filip,
>   i hav ben watching you play. i wood lik to play lik you. i am a king. so i cant.
>   i lik you very much. so rite me and tell me who you ar. i want to get akwainted with you. if your father is in the army they mite allow you to com to the royal garden sumtime to play
>
> —Matthew First

For a time, all goes well. Philip answers the note and is invited by Matthew to help him rule. The two boys manage very well. The spirit of freedom wins over the enemies of the state, but only for a while. Soon, jealous and scheming adults reintroduce corruption, and a plot succeeds in overthrowing the Reformer King, who did so much for the children but never learned how to deal with adults. The beautiful flag he designed for the children of the world—bright green with the white chestnut blossoms of youth at the center—is torn down, and Matt is ban-

A scene from the 1985 Israeli production of *King Matt the First*, by the famous Habima Theater Company RACHEL HIRSCH, RAMAT GAN, ISRAEL

ished to permanent exile on Noman's Isle. He is too good for a bad world.

As Korczak wrote the story, he put a great deal of himself into it. He had founded such utopias in his homes, and while there were problems, they had not been destroyed by the outside world—yet. Korczak realized that the homes could not remain completely separated from the world, no more than King Matt could protect his kingdom forever from sabotage within and evil without.

But in the book, too much love of money and power soon bring down Matt's land despite the children's efforts to fight for it. Then, twenty years later, not in a mythical kingdom—but in Warsaw itself—adult brutality did destroy the orphanages and all they had accomplished, as well as the man who created them.

Children have always responded so deeply to this story that, when the book was first translated into English in 1945, soon after Korczak's death in an extermination camp, the American publisher thought it necessary to insert a special page claiming that Korczak and the orphans had somehow miraculously survived and run away! But in Poland itself, amid the ruins, no one would have believed such a fairy-tale ending. Even children there knew that both the dream state and the man had vanished forever. Today, the only statue of royalty ever built in a Communist country is in the Polish city of Szczecin, where students feed the pigeons that gather on a statue of the little King Matt standing in front of the Janusz Korczak Elementary School.

Two years later, Korczak published another popular book, *When I Am Small Again,* in which a mature teacher and a little boy magically trade places. Each learns what it is like to be the other. The grown-up realizes what is most tiring but demanding about dealing with children: "They are not stupid. It's not the bending down to their level that wears us out—no, it's the reaching up on tiptoe to them that we must do which is so hard."

In Korczak's imagination, adults and children—and he saw himself as both—often changed places to learn from each other. In his theories people learned from being flexible and not standing on ceremony or age. Life was a continual process of education and growth.

Shortly after, in 1926, one of Korczak's best-known projects began when the largest Polish-language Jewish newspaper in Warsaw offered to print for him a six-page supplement folded in as part of its big weekend edition. This "Little Review," as it was called, was produced completely by the children, for the children. Each home already had a newspaper, but no one outside usually read it. Now Korczak's children really had a national voice.

To him, writing had always been of the greatest importance. Many children entered the homes withdrawn and unable to express themselves or to argue for what they believed without violence or tears. "The school paper expresses the conscience of the group and cements its unity. Those who cannot make themselves heard any other way here have the chance to speak and be listened to in peace and quiet," Korczak said.

The "Little Review" was an immediate favorite throughout the country. Fan clubs sprang up. Eventually more than two thousand correspondents from ages six to eighteen wrote articles, essays, news, and poetry. Except for himself as the one adult editor, every job was held by a child. Many had their own desks and secretaries. Subscribers all over Poland waited eagerly for each copy to read their favorite features. And they wrote in—about 10,000 letters a year. Every one was kept, none ever destroyed. The newspaper appeared regularly right up to the time of the Nazi invasion in 1939. Many contributors used their experiences later as professional writers. Korczak himself saw the children's paper as allowing things out of the ordinary to be said: "I would like it to print things that adults will be afraid to read!"

Korczak also wrote another long fairy tale for children in 1924, which was translated into many languages. He was fascinated with the idea of America as he imagined it to be—wide-open spaces and skyscrapers filled with hardworking people living so differently from the tired old ways of Europe that never seemed to change. So he set his new book, *Little Jack Goes Bankrupt*, there, in a make-believe American town.

Like *King Matt*, it shows a good-hearted boy who dreams of reforming the world. With other honest children, he establishes a community store based on truth

and cooperation. But dishonest adults soon spoil everything. Finances collapse and Little Jack, which Korczak
thought was a typical American name, is saved from total
ruin only when his idea for a children's bank is accepted.
He and his friends must go on struggling to be understood
and make changes in the way things have always been
done.

A few years later Korczak explained his idea that a
person has to use his energies wisely so as not to bankrupt them; that is, so as not to run out of strength before
the important battles have been fought. In a letter he
signed Goldszmit, written in 1932 from Warsaw to a
former resident of the home living in Palestine, he explained how important it was to have the right goals in
life:

> If you make your life's aim just "satisfaction" of
> yourself—whether the stomach or the mind—you are
> always in danger of bankruptcy: When everything is
> used up, you get the feeling of hating being full;
> you'd prefer being empty, unfinished.
> But if your aim is to feed others, not just yourself—
> then you have a goal ahead of you; you can melt
> away your own sufferings and bring joy to others by
> escaping from personal ambitions. If you fail then, it
> is painful, yes, but not poisonous. It's not an easy or
> comfortable life, but an honest, straightforward one
> full of daily tasks.

As he grew older, Korczak knew that his childhood
dreams would stay with him always. Like Little Jack, he
would have to do all he could to protect them from the
corruption of the outside world, which blocked any changes
threatening the position of the wealthy and powerful.

Choosing to feed and take care of others rather than himself meant he would never be faced with the feeling of having wasted his time or reached the end of the road. There were always new challenges when one decided to combat the injustices of the world.

15

Sparrows and Swallows

After about ten years of being in charge of both homes, Korczak found himself a famous man in his own country and in the rest of Europe. His books and stories were read in many languages. People came from many countries to observe the working of the Children's Republics and marvel at the honesty and faithfulness to ideals that the children showed. Although conditions in Poland remained very uncertain, the orphanages were oases of security.

Korczak tried to reach as many people as possible with his ideas. He was the favorite professor at the Warsaw Free (Open) University, where restrictions imposed by the government—especially against Jewish students—did not apply. At the official university, liberal students were harassed and politics dominated over learning. Jews were forced to sit apart on ghetto benches, which became a symbol of hatred and humiliation. Years before, Madame Curie, the world-famous scientist, had received much of her education at the Free University, where radical new ideas could be discussed and special groups such as women had opportunities open to them.

He also served as adviser to the Warsaw municipal courts on questions of juvenile crime and probation, as his father had done on divorce matters so many years ago.

Korczak was beloved at the Jewish Teachers Training Institute too, where he lectured on how to introduce better methods into the classroom. Students appreciated his manner of making errors deliberately to allow them to correct him, and of speaking at their own level. He asked them to provide him with experiences from their lives and used these stories in his classes. He was completely different from the other professors, who recited old lectures from notebooks, without ever looking up.

Once he walked into a huge lecture hall with a small child next to him. He put the boy behind a fluoroscope— a screen for observing internal organs—so the audience of twenty-year-olds could see the child's heart beating wildly from nervousness.

After a silence, the doctor told them, "The next time you are about to yell at a child or punish him because you have lost patience, the next time you are even tempted to strike him . . . think of this child and this heart that you see fluttering here. Think of it and stop."

Another time, he arrived late, which was very unusual for him. Many of the other teachers often never showed up for class at all, and the students accepted this as part of their unpredictable behavior, but Korczak was always present and on time. He had too much to tell them to waste a minute.

No one would leave because they knew that he was coming. At last he arrived and calmly explained that he had been engrossed in such an important task at the home that he had lost track of the hour. He had been sorting the children's handkerchiefs: It was another of the small activities that he attended to because he felt he learned a great deal about each child and his values.

Korczak needed such information to achieve his lifetime aim: to be an upbringer and educator of children, though neither a biological parent nor merely a teacher. He combined his medical powers of observation and diagnoses with love, to lead children to a better future and not just reinforce the errors of the past. Having rejected political socialism, he was a true socializer who made it possible for many to live together in peace and understanding.

In the homes, different patterns emerged as the number of children grew. Each year, new ones entered, others left, while some stayed as the experienced nucleus of the group. Every new child was sponsored by a veteran who helped him become oriented to the totally new life. After a month, each child was voted upon by the general population according to a four-point scale of how he had impressed the others with his cooperativeness and desire to belong. With a 1 being the lowest, each child had the rest of the first year to improve his rank. No one could stay past that with a 1.

The doctor helped everyone to improve and emphasized the need for group solidarity and loyalty. He encouraged the children to make bets with him that they would be able to master any of their weak areas. Most responded to this challenge by showing what they could achieve if given recognition: Korczak was forever rummaging in the pockets of his green coverall for treats to pay off a winner. He was delighted to lose every bet, for in fact, the child had won.

One boy bet he could cure himself of using a particularly offensive curse word. After a week, he was down to only fifteen times. He kept wagering on smaller numbers, sometimes winning, sometimes not, but always trying to improve on the previous week. Six weeks later, he was free of the habit completely, and of other curses too. Korczak himself bet—and lost—that he could stop smoking.

Everything was done in the most positive way possible. One winter Korczak received complaints from the city transport company that several of his older boys had abused the honor system on the tramline they rode to school each morning. They were getting in the back of the car and avoided paying by jumping off when their stop came. Many people did this and were seldom caught, but occasionally the authorities would crack down. Recently some of the home children had been seen riding in this way, and from the descriptions given, Korczak knew who they were.

Early one morning, while it was still quite dark, he followed them to the stop without being seen. He was careful so that they didn't even see the steam from his breath in the frigid air. Sure enough, they sneaked in the back door and were happily congratulating themselves when they spotted the doctor in the legal section watching them calmly. All their merriment vanished.

After depositing the correct fares for everyone, he motioned them to get off the tram at the next stop. There was a terrible silence. He led them, surprisingly, into a favorite coffeehouse and pastry shop at the corner and ordered an appetizing assortment for him and them. He urged them to have "more, why don't you?" and said nothing about their behavior except "Don't burn your tongues!" The boys fretted, waiting for him to say something to break the tension. They could barely enjoy the sweets.

Finally the doctor spoke. "What you've been doing is

really small scale, you know, but there is a chance you will get into the habit and slip into stealing bigger things— fruit from the market, then purses, then into jail when you get caught, and you will get caught. I myself never went beyond an apple from a stand, but I never forgot how bad I felt when I did even that.

"Don't get sucked into this, boys, because the world is just waiting to discipline you and then I won't be able to do anything to help. I won't be there to buy your ticket. This could be your last chance. Give me your hands and tell me this is the last time. Shake my hand on it, now, every one of you."

The boys did as he asked and then burst into tears. They had let him down, and he had treated them so well. They felt they owed him the simple pledge he asked for; from that time on, there were no more complaints from the conductors.

Even the nights were full of responsibilities. The doctor and Stefa went around the boys' and girls' rooms to check on each one individually. They covered or uncovered depending on the weather, tucked in a strayed arm or leg. Korczak listened carefully to the patterns of sleep, the breathings and coughs that spoke of health or danger.

"Had it not been for this home, these children would never have known that there were good people on earth, people who do not steal or swear or beat them. They would never have known that it is good to tell the truth, nor would they ever have realized that there are such things as good laws, tenderness, and love," he wrote.

To have any time at all for his writing and lecture planning, he needed to get away from all the duties of running the homes—reading the thousands of thank-you notes the children had to write to one another whenever they performed favors, responding to each of the memos left for him in the open Letters to Pan Doktor box, saving and sorting each bit of work done by every child. He also needed a place apart from the crowded dormitory, yet not so far that he couldn't be reached fast.

So, late at night, after his duties were done, he would go to the attic, where he could be undisturbed. In the day he would occasionally sit there too, feeding his favorite birds, the sparrows. They reminded him of the Polish peasants, always faithfully there, unchanging, like the familiar landscape he loved. "I prefer them to the swallows or the pigeons," he explained, "because swallows leave each year, and we may never see them again."

The children crept up to the attic to be near him, too. Always the scientific observer, he noted from his desk how once in the room, they were always drawn to the freedom of the window he left open for them, to the light and color of the horizon:

> Every day I put an armchair and stool a bit far from the window, and then I watch how the children quietly manage to move themselves back in front of it. Like plants moving toward the light. Even if it's windy, rainy, or cold; it's like the "law" that makes potato shoots climb up the wall of the cellar—the urge that draws humans to look into space.

These quiet moments of nighttime study ("not to know answers, but to ask more questions") were all too rare for Korczak or Stefa, who as usual, assumed most of the practical responsibilities. After a time, she told the children that, at her age, they should begin to call her Mrs. Stefa rather than Miss. This was as far as she apparently ever aspired to a conventional marriage. Even if she and Henryk had been married like other people, how could they ever have had a family such as this? As she said, "I have fifty little girls and fifty little boys. I also have one elder child who's the most difficult of all to manage—Dr. Korczak." Could she have asked for more? In fact, she had never settled for a standard role in anything. She was mother to them all.

16

Divided Loyalties

In the troubled decade of the 1930s, conditions became sharply worse for the future of the two homes. Like all other countries, Poland was hit severely by economic collapse and the worldwide Depression. Both the Soviet Union and Germany, Poland's powerful neighbors and each other's enemies, were in political turmoil that threatened Poland with the possibility of revolution. The old story of domination and conquest seemed ready to repeat itself. How long would Poland stay free this time?

With the increasing dangers from Hitler's Germany, many Poles themselves became more militaristic. Anti-Semitism, the blaming of Jews for the problems of the country, became even more visible, but there was little the Jews could do. Only a certain number could enter Palestine, under British restrictions, and bad economic conditions all over the world meant that it would be even harder to establish a new life anywhere else. In 1936, the vice-president of the parliament said threateningly, "Poland has room for only fifty thousand Jews; the other three million must leave." To patriotic citizens like Korczak and Stefa, all their progress seemed endangered by such talk.

Stefa went on a first visit to Palestine in 1930 and urged Korczak to follow. She was as attached to Poland as he, and she was not strongly Zionist, but she was younger and more flexible. She felt drawn to the new way of life introduced by the early Jewish settlers. The kibbutz united Jews from many backgrounds into a cooperative, shared system rather like a year-round camp. They all worked together and had similar goals. Private profits and ownership were replaced by common labor. Children were cared for by everyone in turn. The kibbutz had both religious and nonreligious Jews. There was room for everyone; to Stefa it seemed perfect.

She stayed for six weeks with settlers there whom she had known when they were children at the home. She worked in the nursery and on the land. She learned modern Hebrew rapidly and could speak with people easily. Although conditions were sometimes primitive and so different from Poland, knowing what was happening at home made Palestine seem like a haven.

Korczak himself sailed there for a visit in 1934. He had to fight against the feeling that he was abandoning the children, even for a short time, but he was convinced he owed it to them to investigate what might be a safe place for them later. The graduates of the home welcomed him like a father, and he was fascinated with the completely new climate, landscape, and desert way of life.

Shortly before, he had written to Joseph Arnon, a former resident of the home who now lived in Palestine, "I have made a definite promise to try life in the Holy Land, but I don't know how it will work. Maybe I'm not

Korczak during trip to Palestine in the 1930s POLISH KOR-
CZAK ASSOCIATION

even entitled to it. I am aware how difficult it is to
converse by means of motions and signs, especially with
children, who are the most important thing to me. . . . And
I have heard that you call the native children Sabras. I
don't understand that. I should like to see them for
myself."

Of course the doctor shouldn't have worried. Even if he wasn't as good as Stefa in learning new languages, he found the children very eager to communicate with him, by signs if necessary. And he learned that the sabra plant was a kind of prickly cactus unknown in Europe. Its fruit was like a porcupine outside but soft and sweet within. The natives called themselves this to show that they were a new breed of Jews, tough and adaptable.

Very soon, Korczak was charmed by the raw new land. He admired the kibbutz system; it was a child of the future too, a noble experiment in changing the old ways and rewriting history. "If there is one place where the child is honestly given a chance to express his dreams and his fears, his longings and doubts—it is possibly the Holy Land. There a monument should be built to the Unknown Orphan."

When he and Stefa were reunited back in Warsaw, they went through one crisis after another. In 1936 he had to resign from Our Home because the anti-Semitic political parties had gained so much strength. He felt terribly cut off from the majority of the children.

For a number of years, he had also been broadcasting on the state radio a highly popular series of friendly talks to the public. But the station had never told the audience who the "Old Doctor from the Radio" was; they were afraid that many Poles would not want to hear advice on child-raising from a Jew. He read stories from the "Little Review" and other newspapers and magazines; both adults and children listened faithfully.

Pressures grew to exclude Jews from public life, and he was forced to end broadcasting, even under his anonymous identity. He was silenced and felt betrayed by his nation, but was helpless to protest publicly.

Stefa had gone to Palestine again, and after she returned, he went there too, badly depressed, for a much longer stay in 1936. He traveled throughout the tiny country, seeing new child-care facilities that were so close in spirit to what he hoped to do in Poland one day. He learned how people encouraged children to get up on time by putting a rooster in the room to crow or gently pouring water on their heads! The idea of staying forever grew much stronger:

> What is important is that at first I want to seclude myself for a year in Jerusalem and start, as if I were a kindergarten child myself, to adjust to a different climate, language, and life. It's hard when one is sixty. . . .
>
> The menace that hovers over me in Europe is the fate of a sour, bitter old man, a loser, as the children would say. But here will I succeed in being born anew? This is my last try. Is it too late? No—had I gone earlier, I would have felt like a deserter. One has to remain at one's duty until the very last minute.

Korczak found himself terribly divided in his loyalties. He surely saw the dangers in Europe, although he would never admit that Poland, rather than Germany, was going to harm him and the home. He sensed that this was really the last chance, but he was afraid of longing for home forever if he took the step and emigrated. And his worst fear was what would happen to the children he would have to leave behind. Clearly they could not all come.

His mind wavered back and forth. He decided he would return to Poland and visit Palestine for a part of each year. He planned to become more of a Zionist and to educate the young Polish Jews to work toward emigrating in the future by preparing and strengthening themselves now. He continued corresponding with his friends in Palestine, who urged him to come back. At the Kibbutz Ein Harod, which he and Stefa loved because it was one of the oldest and was surrounded by pines, palms, and eucalyptus trees sweetening the air, they kept a Korczak corner. His favorite armchair, in which he had sat and peeled potatoes, is still there. His friends had wanted him to take it back to Warsaw, but he had refused, saying he never wished to become a slave to his possessions.

Stefa had made another trip but returned to Poland very soon before war actually started on September 1, 1939, to try to get the doctor to come with her one last time. She had become accustomed to living in Palestine, but her heart was torn between the two lands. How could she leave Henryk and the children at their moment of greatest need? She had chosen a long time before to love him and to devote her life to him and his dreams. While he had said many times that "the only place for a Jewish child these days is in a Jewish land," he was clearly incapable of leaving them behind.

Less than one month before the war started, he had written to Joseph Arnon with real hope:

> July was a wonderful month—twenty new children I discovered, like twenty books written in a new language barely known, like books slightly damaged, pages missing, puzzles and riddles. Just like the old days—things that are important are lost sandals, a thorn in the foot, a quarrel over the swing, a broken branch. I slept in the isolation room with the children who had the measles. I kept myself awake listening to their breathing, coughing, and sighing. What wisdom there is in their sleep. . . . If I have enough money, I'll come for a four-month visit, October to January.

Up to the day the war started, he and Stefa spoke of taking the children to safety in Palestine. He called it a "possible second League of Nations," with Jerusalem a world center for spiritual rebirth. He was aware, too, of

Korczak with members of the staff POLISH KORCZAK
ASSOCIATION

the dangers and uncertainties they might find and was
hesitant to expose the children to the unknown. When he
was totally honest, he was afraid that "in Palestine it's
bound to be the same—the sadness of children, the antics
of adult animals. What the world really needs is not
orange groves but a new faith in the future and in the
child as the source of all hope."

He was very proud of what they had accomplished in
Poland. A survey of the children who had lived in the
Orphans' Home in its first years of existence from 1912 to
1932 showed remarkable results. "Out of 455, just two
have become beggars, two prostitutes, and three convicted
of theft." The remaining 98 percent, all from the worst
possible conditions, had fulfilled his hopes for them.

His writings were increasingly famous, too. He received

praise for his new play, *The Senate of Madmen*, a grim fantasy set in an insane asylum that represented Europe on the eve of war. In the play, the old ghosts of his past—madness, suicide, despair—come back and threaten to overwhelm man. In the homes, the children had shown they could rule without interference and maintain justice, but in the adult world, a Senate of Madmen seemed to be running things.

In 1938, he also wrote a story, "The Tale of Hersh" (his own Jewish name). In it, a little boy is frightened when he hears a prediction of God's planned destruction of the Jews. But out of fear, the words God wrote fly away and hide in Heaven. At the last minute, the Jews are spared.

As an old man tells a boy in *The Senate of Madmen*, "When God abandons man, He goes back to heaven. Then He returns one day in a shower of pearls that fall right into the hearts of children. You, the child, are our only hope."

Very soon, however, Korczak, Stefa, and many others—adults and children—were to feel utterly abandoned by God and their fellow man. Only with the greatest difficulty could they find any room for hope, any chance for survival. The impossible was about to occur.

17

Into the District of the Damned

When the German invasion of Poland began in 1939, the situation for the Jews of Europe was very different from what it had been in the past. Now there was an enemy who had openly proclaimed his hatred for them specifically—and his intention to remove them forever as a problem to the rest of the world. Now that the war had actually broken out, within Germany itself and in all countries it conquered, the Jews suffered immediately.

Warsaw was bombarded for several weeks, starting on September 1, and thousands of civilians, including three thousand Jews, were killed. It wasn't coincidental that the heaviest bombings took place on the Jewish holidays and in the Jewish districts. The struggle was over in a few weeks despite fierce fighting. The city lay in ruins from the new and devastating air warfare. Before starting the invasion, Hitler had made a special pact with Russia to divide up Poland between them: Now this was done and free Poland died again.

But along with the land, Germany inherited millions of unwanted Jews. No one had any doubt what the Germans intended to do. In the area around Warsaw, they established a new government under their absolute rule. Any Jew who could fled to the east into the new Russian zone, into at least the chance of safety. But most stayed in their homes, helpless.

Korczak put on his Polish army uniform and broadcast appeals on the radio for the soldiers to resist the invaders. During one lunch hour, while the children sat at the table in the home, a huge explosion shook the building. A boy ran out to see.

"Pan Doktor," he cried rushing back inside covered with brick dust. "A bomb landed in the courtyard and blew a great big hole in the ground. Come look, come look; it just missed the rabbit cages!"

The doctor went out cautiously and came back a few minutes later, holding his cap gingerly in his hand. The force of the explosion had sucked it out of the window near where he had left it lying. "Well," he said in a curiously shaky voice, "it seems as if the Germans want me to keep my bald head covered and also help us replant the courtyard a bit: They made a nice big hole for us to put in a big chestnut tree. Back to your meal, children."

At first his knowledge of German helped the doctor run the home. He went to the new headquarters in his uniform to request more food supplies because now things were becoming scarce and he had many hungry mouths to feed. But he refused to wear a Jewish star on his arm as the Nazis had decreed. To him, this represented a step back centuries into history. When the Nazis realized that this doctor was a Jew, they began abusing him for not following the new orders. "I've fought in four wars, and I never wore any emblems on myself then. Why should I, a Polish doctor, have to now?"

He was beaten and imprisoned for several months. All

the while, the children flew a flag at half-mast in the courtyard, and Stefa sought help. Finally, some former residents of the home raised a large sum and bought his freedom on the grounds that he was insane, for who else would have spoken like that to the Germans? He emerged a different man. Now he knew that hope was gone and what the future held for them.

The real nightmare took shape in 1940 when the Germans decided to make a bombed-out part of the central city, where many Jews had lived before the war, into a totally Jewish zone. To do this, they ordered over 200,000 people to move: non-Jews out, Jews from everywhere in. When the great shift was over in a few weeks, about 2 percent of Warsaw had become a closed trap in which a full one-third of its population—almost 500,000 Jews— were caught as in the most terrible ghettos of the past. But those had been areas in which they could live and grow; this was to be a killing ground for their destruction.

Next the Jews were made to work on and pay for building a wall ten feet tall and two bricks wide around the limits set by the Nazis. What had been an open Jewish neighborhood was now a closed, jam-packed reservation. Its area was like a very small town or district in a city that could be easily walked around. There were two parts connected by a footbridge over a busy street that was not part of the ghetto, where other Poles would jeer at those trapped inside. Altogether the ghetto measured about ten blocks on each side, a total of a little more than one square mile—"the District of the Damned."

In most parts of the world, a few thousand people at most might live in such an area. Even big cities, such as Warsaw before the war, had nothing like this concentration of people—up to seven or eight, even a dozen, per room. Today, rebuilt Warsaw has an average of about 8,000 people per square mile, crowded Manhattan has

Jews being forced to build the walls of the Warsaw
Ghetto YIVO INSTITUTE FOR JEWISH RESEARCH

64,000, and the most jammed city in the world, Manila, in the Philippines, has 108,000. But the Nazis forced almost 500,000 Jews into the square mile—and none could legally get out.

To understand how desperate the conditions were, imagine that all the people who come and go each day in a city like New York or Tokyo were suddenly taken prisoner by an enemy and told they could never leave again. If everything they needed for life were to be taken from them and they were permitted to work just enough to survive—such was the state of the Jews in the Warsaw Ghetto. Only a very few were treated better if they promised to help the Nazis by controlling their own people.

The Germans saw to it that life was next to impossible under the official rations allowed. Jews were permitted 184 calories a day while the Germans could have a normal 2,300. For their tiny amount of food (four loaves of bread a month mixed with sawdust and potato peels) the Jews had to pay the equivalent of one dollar per day, while the Nazis paid six cents. Just to survive, the Jews had to smuggle in four times what was allowed, often using children, who climbed the walls or went through holes, risking certain death. To maintain life was now the greatest challenge of all.

Into this nightmare, the Nazis herded tens of thousands of Jews from the areas around Warsaw and other European nations they had conquered. To them, all Jews were a danger to the Christian population and had no right to exist. Whatever happened to them as a result of being kept in such inhuman conditions was of no interest to the Nazis. By their logic, the Jews deserved this fate; the sooner they were removed as anything but a source of slave labor, the better.

This was the conclusion of more than one thousand years of Jewish life in Poland. Over the next four years, no one came to the aid of the masses caught in the ghetto. Today, nothing at all remains of what had been the Jewish cultural center of the world. The few survivors of the war have long since scattered, and since there are almost no children left, in the next century it is possible there will be no more Jews in Poland. Along with countless others, Korczak, Stefa, and the children faced this future as the walls rose around them.

Outside the ghetto, Polish Christians suffered too, because the Nazis considered them an inferior race as well. However, they could move about the rest of the city as they wished, manage a living, and go to sleep expecting that they might live. The Jews were in an entirely different world, completely dependent upon their sworn enemy for food, water, medicine—every element of life that could be taken away for no reason.

After the walls were completed and all windows facing out blocked off, the Nazis declared it a crime punishable by death to leave the ghetto without a special pass, which was almost impossible to get. They reduced the ghetto even further, closed off most of the exit points originally included, and watched as the death toll—especially of the old, the young, and the sick—reached thousands per month.

Day by day, the strongest remaining were rounded up for slave labor outside. Family structure disappeared as each person became a separate unit marked for destruction. With Germany ruling most of Europe through 1942, the Nazis had plenty of time to wait as the ghetto became one huge cemetery, just as they planned.

Korczak had been in other terrible situations before, but none like this. Now he was old and sick. He suffered greatly from swollen legs, kidney and heart disorders, and painful troubles with his eyes and teeth. He had no financial resources left, since the Nazis had seized everything. Mrs. Falska and other loyal friends on the outside

Children in the ghetto   YIVO INSTITUTE FOR JEWISH
RESEARCH

sent word that they could arrange safe-conduct passes for
him to escape and be hidden in relative safety, but this
would have meant, to him, the final betrayal.

"You do not leave a child at night who is sick or in
need. I have two hundred orphans; in a time like this I
will stay by them every minute."

In the ghetto, there were at least 100,000 children, the
majority abandoned or orphaned. The streets were filled
with the most heartbreaking sights of little girls and boys
wandering about, often carrying babies, looking for relatives or food. There were around thirty orphanages or
shelters, and Korczak's was just one. But since his was so
famous, he was continually under pressure to take in
more. Everyone seemed to know of other needy cases.

He and Stefa now recognized that they had turned their
backs on escape to Palestine when it had still been
possible. The last letter received from her by friends was

sent out in 1940 through the Red Cross, and speaks about plans to bring the children to Palestine when the war was over, but this was before the ghetto was finally sealed. After that, they all were no more than living tombstones. The great gap between Jews and Christians had become a permanent distance never to be crossed again.

The doctor now spoke of works he would never have the chance to write:

Children of the Bible, King David the Second—books that will never be. And another one, a new hero I'll call by my own Jewish name, Hersh. He'll be healthy and handsome, a David who will fight the huge Goliath. I have a new flag for him, like King Matthew's, but this one won't just have blossoms on the green for hope, it'll have another side, pure white with a blue Star of David. This will be the last work of a doctor whose own heart is sick.

18

The Ghetto

The Orphans' Home could not stay on Krochmalna Street, where Korczak and Stefa had created their ideal world. Their part of the street was outside the boundaries of the ghetto, so everything had to be left behind. Without looking back, Korczak scouted everything that was available and found a building the children could share with a dozen families. It had been a technical college before the war; its large lecture hall was soon filled with cots and the few possessions the children carried with them.

The actual move was done to raise their spirits as much as possible. To avoid the atmosphere of a juvenile prison, they brought along colored pictures cut from magazines and geranium planters found in the rubble. The doctor told them to pretend they were a theatrical troupe or a circus marching to attract customers. Each child took a lamp, a pillow, perhaps a birdcage, and held it high. The healthy carried the lame on their backs; those who had dreamed of being acrobats now had their chance. They hoped in this way to show the Nazis that they were strong and could work. Everyone knew what had already happened to those the Germans called unfit.

Money for food—even finding the food itself—became a constant nightmare to Korczak. No matter how simply they had lived in the past, this was completely different. Now they were being starved, deliberately, and he alone could prevent it. He wrote open letters to every Jew in the ghetto. He went every day down a different street, to anyone he knew who still had money or something valuable. Some Jews had in fact been profiting from hoarding and a few were even rich from smuggling or dealing in black-market goods with the Germans. Korczak knew these people and went to them to shame them into giving him money. He who had always dreaded meeting beggars and had lectured them to work, not stand with their hands idly out—now he was a beggar asking criminals to feed his children.

While deaths rose from starvation and epidemics, he at least was able to provide a slice of bread, boiled cabbage, wheat mixed with horse's blood, maybe a beet or turnip. He tried everything—abandoned packages of spoiled goods left at the post office, cast-off things found in the street. Anything could be used to keep a child busy or fed one day longer.

He made sure the children kept up their lessons, too. Many artists and musicians, scientists and professors, were trapped in the ghetto, and Korczak went to them and asked them to come to the home to teach or perform. A rich cultural life went on along with regular lessons, to the very end.

There was even bitter humor. A teacher is reported to have asked one boy, "What would you like to be if you were Hitler's son?" The child's answer was, "An orphan."

Korczak witnessed terrible scenes every day. Dying

parents entrusted their children's lives to him because they had heard that he alone was still offering a chance to survive in dignity. Often a mother's or father's last words were whispered into his ears. His children, formerly pitied, now were considered lucky to be in a safe place.

The doctor even found time to help the most desperate cases. There was an open shelter on Dzielna Street where the most hopeless children were left to die. Whatever money existed to care for them was stolen by the starving. Soon it made little difference if the dying were brought in or left outside. Even those hardened by life in the ghetto were shocked and sickened, but who could help?

Korczak—with all his accomplishments—actually applied to the Germans for the job of reorganizing the shelter, which he described to friends as a "slaughterhouse, a mortuary where corpses crawl." He sent the authorities a picture of himself. It shows an aged and ailing man. He humbly filled out a form listing his experiences as a doctor and administrator of orphanages. He listed his name as Goldszmit and his religion as Jewish. He concluded by asking for only a corner of the building to work in for a trial period—as if there were other candidates for the job—and whatever food they had. Even that he said he could do without. For the children themselves, he had only ground-up chalk to stop the diarrhea that was wasting them away.

Back in the new quarters of the home, he acted, for the children's sake, as hopeful as he could. Together with the other families, he organized a few concerts and poetry readings. To their surprise he insisted that Yiddish, not Polish, be used. One song, "Brothers," became an unofficial anthem the children often recited to piano accompaniment.

White and brown and black and yellow,
Mingle the colors together.
All human beings are brothers and sisters,
From one father and one mother.

He also arranged for open Jewish services—no tickets needed—in the holidays of fall 1941. Although he was still known as a great assimilationist, he prayed loudly and even sang in a bit of Hebrew he had learned. He cried when he saw the cantor wheeling in his crippled wife in a baby carriage—how could she be left behind?

On one occasion, he read some satirical writings to an audience seated under the blacked-out windows of the home. When someone accused him of provoking the Germans by poking fun, he replied, "What have we to lose now? We're all Jews here, all together, just as they wished. What more can they do?"

Later, the Germans made the ghetto even smaller, and Korczak had to leave the cramped quarters on Chlodna Street, where they hadn't even been able to separate the boys from the girls. This time they could find only an empty place in an arcade between two busy streets at the south end of the ghetto. In smaller rooms, more and more children had to be taken in. Again Korczak had to move the hundreds of boxes saved from the Children's Court and Parliament on Krochmalna Street, the records of every child's height and weight over the years: He was still planning to write the full history of his experiences taking care of thousands of children. Some few of these papers were found lying about after the war; the great majority were burned as useless trash.

In one room at the last location of the home, mirrors still covered the walls around what had been a dance floor. The doctor dreaded seeing the scrawny bodies reflected all day, further reminders of their hunger and his inability, for the first time, to satisfy it.

19

Racing with Death

Conditions worsened throughout 1941. More than forty thousand people—about 10 percent of the population— died that year. Within a decade, if not sooner, the Nazis' plans for an empty ghetto would be realized. As winter approached, there were no fuels at all for heat, and one important source of help was cut off when the United States entered the war against Germany. Packages had been arriving from abroad from relief agencies, but now the ghetto was completely cut off. In early 1942, secret plans were made in Germany for the total destruction of Jews worldwide. A few months later the Nazis began to suffer losses in important battles, and they hurried to do away with Jews by force and not let time take its toll.

With this aim in mind, they constructed a new death camp for the ghetto at a small town, Treblinka, about an hour away by train, along the main line from Warsaw to Russia, an area of heavy Jewish population. Gas chambers disguised as shower rooms were built, and crematoria to burn the bodies and destroy all evidence. The Jews were told they were being evacuated or resettled to the east; at all costs they were not told the truth.

If they knew, they might rebel, and the Germans could not spare soldiers to fight against them because their army was bogged down, policing the countries they had conquered. The Nazis recruited local populations to help in the extermination process—Poles, Russians, Ukrainians, others—promising them the Jews' possessions. Hitler was eager to get rid of the huge Jewish population he still controlled, so he could concentrate his energy on defeating the Russians.

In spring 1942, Korczak decided that it was finally time to write his personal recollections. He had often thought of leaving behind a diary or memoirs, but where would he find the time to organize his thoughts out of the thousands of pages he had gathered since 1912?

But now, with who knew how little time left and only a fraction of the strength he once had, he was determined to leave something for the world to know him and what he had wanted to do. For three months he put down memories, observations, criticisms, and even a few plans. At the very end, when he knew he would be deported, he arranged, through a trusted friend, to seal the notebook in a wall at the Christian home he had founded with Maryna Falska. Years later it was discovered, saved, and published; it has made him famous again in the world.

Although he knew what the Nazis intended to do—and had already done—he expresses not a word of hate or bitterness in the *Ghetto Diary*. Instead, he concentrates on making things better as they presently are, not trying to change what cannot be undone. Reports had begun to reach the Jews that the German war campaign was not succeeding as it had in the past, but this did not mean that help was coming their way. They still seemed cut off from the whole world.

Worse yet, they had also heard from a few haunted souls who had actually escaped extermination at Treblinka by crawling out of mass graves or playing dead, but no one would believe that murders could be organized on such a scale. They thought the people had gone mad or were seeking sympathy. There had to be some explanation for what was happening. Surely the Germans would find a use for them, each person thought to himself.

Half-believing, half-doubting, Korczak had refused offers of help to escape because he would not leave behind Stefa, the few other adults who worked there, or any of the children. He wouldn't disband the home and try to hide the orphans one by one, either. He hoped that together they might be able to protect one another.

In the *Diary*, Korczak describes his dreams of going one day to America, where he had once hoped to address vast audiences and find the streets paved with gold that he could take back to Poland. No matter where, he still hoped to find a new world where power would not be an excuse for murder. If somehow it became possible to survive the war without surrendering his ideals, he could lead the children to adulthood in a world where they might make a difference. He never stopped believing that they held the key:

> If our bodies live forever, they can do so only through our children. Our spirits can also last forever by radiating the ideal of brotherhood, but not if our bodies look upon death as an end. In fact, it might be a continuation of life in a different form. Our bodies *may* live forever in green grass or a cloud—we just don't know. . . . What we can know is this: Our children, and theirs, may go on. . . . I would only like to be conscious when I die. I want to be able to tell the children "Good-bye" and wish them freedom to choose their own way.

But on a day-to-day basis, even to imagine such ideas, he needed raw alcohol mixed with hot water, a poor substitute for vodka. His body and mind one long ache, only a hot drink could give him sleep or short peace from visions such as he described in his *Diary* on May 29:

> The body of a boy lies on the sidewalk. Is he dead or alive? Nearby three others are playing horses and drivers. At one point they notice the body so they move a few steps to the side and go on playing. Then their reins get tangled and they stumble over him. One says, "Let's get out of here; he's just in the way." They move on.

Korczak, too, had to learn to look the other way. How many people could one worn-out man help?

> I am so very tired. When I wake up in the morning, it is even an effort to think. Getting up means I must raise myself into a sitting position. It means reaching for underwear and buttoning it up. If not all, at least one button. Fighting with my shirt. In order to put on socks, bending down. Then suspenders . . . What exhausting work!

For a time, he kept handy a few pills to bring his sufferings to an end: a fast shove of the glass capsule into his mouth, a bite down, and in a minute or two the convulsions that would give the Germans another victory. But then what would become of the children? How could he now, after all these years, give in to despair and suicide? He threw away the poison and decided for life— with the children—to the end.

20

The Final Destination

By July 1942, the number of Jews in the ghetto had declined through starvation and disease to around 380,000, but the Nazis kept finding new prisoners to send in. Clearly, more drastic steps were needed to empty the ghetto faster: On July 22, Korczak's sixty-fourth birthday, the authorities were informed that large shipments of people were going to be sent to Treblinka daily, beginning immediately. The president of the Jewish community realized that the beginning of the end had come; he took poison while sitting at his desk.

One of the legends relating to Korczak's last weeks of life says that the soldier who had to bring him the news to begin to get the children ready for resettlement had been an orphan himself at the Christian home many years before. He was sent to Germany for adoption by a distant relative there and later rose in the German army. The story says that he was chosen by the High Command to give false reassurance to Korczak because they had known each other. The soldier was in fact found to have committed suicide the day after Korczak and the children were deported on August 5. Had he been able to tell them outright what lay ahead? Or had he lied?

In any event, at the end of July everyone knew that time had run out; the ghetto had to disappear. First the Jews had been rushed in—now they were being hurried out, thousands every day, to death.

As a final event to raise spirits, Korczak decided to put on a performance of the children's play *The Post Office*, by Rabindranath Tagore, a mystical Indian writer and philosopher. He sent invitations throughout what remained of the ghetto and signed them with both his names—Goldszmit/Korczak. The two parts of his life were now one as he faced the coming challenge of the Nazi plan for the final removal of the Jews.

It was important that a large audience attend so that he could collect as much as possible from anyone who had money left to give. The children made patched but clean costumes from even older scraps of clothing than they normally wore. One of the stronger boys played the lead role, Amal, a dying Indian child who learns at the end that the Angel of Death will finally come to take him peacefully back to Nature. The room was filled with sobs. Although many adults cried to see the children bravely recite their lines, Korczak took hope that the experience would help them be stronger for the ordeal they might face any day.

The Nazi timetable called for about six thousand Jews to be taken each day from the streets and brought to the station, where they were packed into wagons built for cattle. Since most were so thin from years of neglect, more could be crowded in, perhaps one hundred jammed together with no seats, no windows, no toilets—nothing but their shared terror. One or two trains of up to forty wagons were sent to Treblinka per day, and returned empty to Warsaw.

At the extermination center, within a few hours all were gassed without knowing until the final minutes what was happening. Everything was disguised: Behind the first-aid sign, an armed guard shot anyone who opened the door looking for help. In August 1942, about 135,000 Jews were killed there, sometimes as many as 10,000 a day when the shipments were very full. In all of Europe, in that month alone, 400,000 Jews were killed at the various camps built with the most modern equipment for this purpose.

There were doctors there, too—the opposite of Korczak—experts in death, not life. They were most concerned with finding new ways of suffering, not curing. And they were often cruelest to the children, the next generation they had to destroy.

After a time, the workers who thought they would be saved had to be killed too. No one could remain sane there for long. The Nazis were determined that nobody know or be able to tell what happened at Treblinka. In the year that it functioned at top speed, almost all the Jews of Warsaw and many others from elsewhere perished. No precise records were kept, but historians estimate that more than three-quarters of a million were put to death.

August 5 was the date chosen for the liquidation of the orphanages and the capture of all stray children. The Nazi plan was to dispose of the most defenseless first. The day before, Korczak wrote in his *Diary*, with no indication that he knew these were to be his last recorded words:

I am watering the flowers. My bald head in the window makes a splendid target. The German soldier has a rifle; he stands and looks so calmly. Perhaps he too was a village schoolmaster or a street sweeper or waiter in civilian life.

What would he do if I nodded to him? Waved my hand in a friendly gesture?

Perhaps he doesn't even know that things are as they are. He may have arrived only yesterday, from far away. . . .

This soldier may have been part of the special roundup squad that came the next morning, sealed off the street, and barked out orders for everyone to get out and line up in the courtyard. But closing the exits and waving guns about were apparently not necessary: Eyewitness accounts, found after the war, report that calm and order prevailed. Korczak and Stefa had prepared the children for whatever might happen.

They came out of the building carrying their new flag— green with white blossoms and the blue Star of David— just as Korczak had designed it. Each carried a few belongings in one hand—perhaps a toy shovel or beach pail ready for the outing—and held on to another child with the other. They walked in double file for the next hour on their last mile.

The final stop was the station at the other end of the ghetto. It was unusually hot, but the doctor rallied his strength and carried the smallest child in his arms as he walked. Stefa was with the older children at the rear. Afterward, Korczak's green smock and his cracked glasses were found back at the home. He knew he would not need them.

As they passed a street leading to the old Jewish cemetery, Korczak is reported to have told the Nazi officer marching alongside, "You could save a bit of time, you know, by sending us off right there"—pointing to the graveyard, where unburied bodies lay, the thousands dying being too much for the gravediggers. "Why not end the trip here, now?"

But the march went on, through streets usually full of noise and frantic activity, now ghostly quiet. Onlookers knew what was happening but were afraid to make a sound for fear the Nazis would shoot. The doorways and windows were filled with people with handkerchiefs pressed to their mouths. Tears flowed, but apparently not from the children.

Concerning the final destination itself, a member of the Jewish police who was forced to work that day has left his report:

> We put the children from the home at the far end of the square, hoping to save them that way at least until the afternoon or maybe the next day. I suggested to Korczak that he come with me to the headquarters of the Ghetto and ask for help. He refused because he wouldn't leave them even for that short time, not even for a minute. He feared a trick and that he might be separated from them. We couldn't convince him.
>
> Then the Germans began loading the train. I watched with my heart in my mouth hoping that my plan might work. But there was still room for more inside. Urged on by whips, more and more were packed in.
>
> Suddenly the brute in charge ordered the children to be brought forward. Korczak was at the head. I'll never forget that sight until the end of my life. The heads held high, a silent protest against the murderers. All the Jewish police saluted them and snapped to attention.
>
> "Who is that man?" asked the Germans.

The story is that, at the last moment, the German commander recognized Korczak as the famous author whose books he had loved as a child, and offered the doctor a delay in deportation or even safety for himself if he would let the children go on alone. Korczak, or Goldszmit the Jew, as the Nazis saw him, could be useful in the coming days to help reassure and get the masses of Jews ready. Others say that a note arrived from the German authorities telling the guards to release him, but it was too late.

No matter what actually occurred, it is sure that Korczak stood at his full height as he stepped into the boxcar. Carefully, he helped the others climb in, putting himself at the center and being sure that each child had a place to stand. Stefa, the laundress, the seamstress, and the other adults joined them. They waited with dignity for the doors to be closed and sealed, then for the train to start up. The last recorded sight of him, then as in his whole life, was of a solitary man comforting the children.

Afterword

At several of the sites of extermination camps in Poland, there are memorials to the vanished communities. Treblinka today is a peaceful town again, and it is hard to imagine the terrible events that took place there. The Nazis recorded only the numbers of people killed, not names. We know that in the first deportations of August 1942, sometimes fifteen thousand arrived in a day. Korczak, Stefa, and the children were among them. By the end of the year, the ground at Treblinka became heavy with 35,000 tons of bodies.

In April 1943, when there were about fifty thousand Jews left in the Warsaw Ghetto, a serious revolt broke out. The Jews knew that the Nazis intended to kill every one of them and then bulldoze the area, so a small band decided to fight rather than be taken.

For six weeks they succeeded in holding off a much larger number of soldiers and calling the attention of the world to their situation. Nonetheless almost every one was killed or found in bombed-out sewers and then executed. Others jumped to their deaths from smoking roofs. The Nazi commander, Jurgen Stroop, finally was able to proclaim on May 16 that the last of the "Jewish cowards, bandits, and thugs—the scum of humanity—" had been captured and that "the Jewish quarter of Warsaw is no more!"

The square mile was, in fact, totally destroyed by bombing from the ground up, until nothing at all remained. After the war it was rebuilt as a modern residential area, with a statue to commemorate what had occurred. As the Nazis intended, the Jews were finally gone, forever.

At Treblinka, large jagged stones and boulders stand as memorials to the Jews and others who died there. Cities, towns, villages, and nations are represented—sometimes the rock stands for a few, other times for hundreds of

The immense devastation that was the Warsaw Ghetto, seen immediately after the war   YIVO INSTITUTE FOR JEWISH RESEARCH

A group of Polish scouts commemorate the exterminations at Treblinka. They are shown around the stone erected to honor Korczak and the children. This is the only stone at the camp to bear an individual's name rather than that of a town or community. POLISH KORCZAK ASSOCIATION

thousands. Only one has a person's name: "Janusz Korczak (Henryk Goldszmit) and the Children."

This rock and the shadow it casts cannot speak of Korczak's accomplishments. No single stone could tell his story, and although Poland, Israel, and other countries have named schools and hospitals for him, the brutality of war erased his presence forever. His ideals live on only through the efforts of scholars and associations dedicated to his memory. Today, too, an asteroid, or small planet, bears his name. A Russian astronomer discovered it between Mars and Jupiter in 1971. Ten years later, Minor Planet 2163 was officially called Korczak.

Some have said that if he could be known as a Jew in Poland and a Pole in Israel, he would consider that, at least, a great victory for mankind.

Above all, Korczak showed what he called a teacher's love in action. He knew that a person could be as good only as he acted, not just thought or spoke. Ideas and theories counted for nothing if adults didn't practice what they said. Socialism, pacifism—all had to work for a better life.

As a teacher, he had to think well of himself first, act as an example for the children to look up to and copy. It did no one any good to have a sentimental idea of a perfect child, kept in a never-never land and then expected to cope with life unprepared. On the contrary, honesty and frankness in facing the problems children would have as adults could help them survive the constant struggle of weak and strong.

Like physical labor, a teacher's love was hard work. It asked much of the children but more of the adult. It made Korczak and Stefa and the others associated with them unusual persons—they would not have wanted to be called heroes—who believed that every child should also want to be unusual. If their aim still comes true one day, then the forces of hatred and oppression haven't a chance against the power of the individual.

JANUSZ KORCZAK
1878–1942

Korczak's Works in English

Big Business Billy [adaptation of *Little Jack Goes Bankrupt*]. Translated by Cyrus Brooks. London: Minerva Publishing Company, 1939.

Ghetto Diary. Translated by Jerzy Bachrach and Barbara Krzywicka. With "The Last Walk of Janusz Korczak" by Aaron Zeitlin, translated by Hadassah Rosensaft and Gertrude Hirschler. New York: Holocaust Library, 1978.

King Matt the First [first published in 1923]. Translated by Richard Lourie. New York: Farrar, Straus, and Giroux, 1986.

Selected Works of Janusz Korczak. Edited by Martin Wolins, translated by Jerzy Bachrach. Published in Poland for the National Science Foundation, Washington, D.C., 1967.

Index

Italic page numbers refer to captions.